Shanghaied

DATE DUE

JUN 2 1986			
OCT 3 0 1997			
JAN 0 5 1998			
JAN 0 5			
JUN 1 9 2008			

DEMCO

Trailblazer Books

Shanghaied
—to—
China

DAVE & NETA JACKSON

Text Illustrations by
Julian Jackson

BETHANY HOUSE PUBLISHERS
MINNEAPOLIS, MINNESOTA 55438

Inside illustrations by Julian Jackson.
Cover design and illustration by Catherine Reishus McLaughlin.

All Scripture quotations are from the King James Version of the Bible.

Published by Bethany House Publishers
A Ministry of Bethany Fellowship, Inc.
11300 Hampshire Avenue South
Minneapolis, Minnesota 55438

Printed in the United States of America

Library of Congress Cataloging-in-Publication Data

Jackson, Dave.
    Shanghaied to China / Dave & Neta Jackson ; text illustrations by
Julian Jackson.
       p. cm. — (Trailblazer)
    Summary: When he is taken aboard a ship bound for China, twelve-
year-old Neil Thompson is befriended by Hudson Taylor and shares
adventures with him during the voyage and in China, where Taylor
sets up a mission.

    [1. Missionaries—Fiction. 2. Taylor, James Hudson, 1832–
1905—Fiction. 3. China—Fiction. 4. Christian life—Fiction.
5. Sea stories.] I. Jackson, Neta. II. Jackson, Julian, ill. III. Title.
IV. Series.
PZ7.J132418Sh   1993
[Fic]—dc20   93–32552
ISBN 1–55661–271–0   CIP
                                            AC
                                         Rev

All the named adult characters in this book and their experiences are real. However, British records identify only the captain and not the crew members of the ship *Dumfries*. Therefore, we made up the names of the first mate and the black steward. For the sake of the story, the order of some events has been altered, and the time in China has been compressed to one year, when the events actually occurred over Hudson Taylor's first two and a half years of ministry in that country.

Hudson Taylor's courtship of Maria Dyer occurred essentially as described in this story, though the location was in Ningpo, a city south of Shanghai.

Neil Thompson and Yang Namu and their specific interactions with Hudson Taylor and other characters are fictional, though Taylor's servant did rob him while on a trip to the interior.

DAVE AND NETA JACKSON are a husband/wife writing team who have authored or coauthored many books on marriage and family, the church, and relationships, including *On Fire for Christ: Stories from Martyrs Mirror*, the Pet Parables series, and the Caring Parent series.

They have three children: Julian, the illustrator for the Trailblazer series, Rachel, on a short-term mission to Honduras, and Samantha, their high school Cambodian foster daughter. They make their home in Evanston, Illinois, where they are active members of Reba Place Church.

CONTENTS

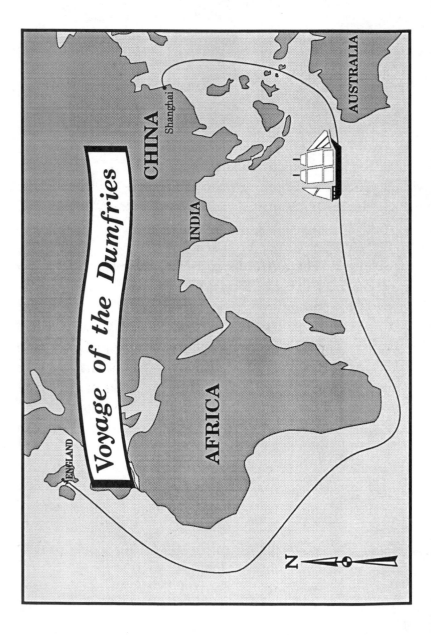

Voyage of the Dumfries

ENGLAND

AFRICA

INDIA

CHINA
Shanghai

AUSTRALIA

N

Chapter 1

Knocked on the Head

I AWOKE IN A STRANGE BED, and then it came to me: it was September 19, 1853, and I was in Liverpool, England. But I also remembered with a sinking disappointment that Grandfather Thompson was sick in bed and couldn't take me down to the docks.

Only my grandmother had met me at the train the night before. After a big hug, she explained, "I know, Neil, that coming from the country you have your heart set on seeing the ships tomorrow, but you'll just have to wait until the captain feels better."

"That's all right. I can wait," I assured her, but in the morning I didn't feel so patient.

My grandfather was a sea captain, and since he had spent most of his life out to sea, I'd only seen him once before. But now that he had retired, he'd invited me to come stay with him and Grandmother for a while. "I'll show you all the ships in port and introduce you to every captain," his letter had promised.

But now he was sick.

I got out of bed and looked out the small round window. It was just like a porthole in a ship. A lot of things in my grandparents' house came from ships or the sea. There were brightly polished brass lanterns outside the front door, a big shell and a spyglass on the mantel, and a map of the world on the wall. The beams of the ceilings in the rooms were low and dark, and the "handrail" up the narrow stairs to the little room where I slept was nothing but a fat rope. I loved it all. Someday I wanted to go to sea, too.

The morning was bright but foggy. From my window the roofs of the neighboring houses seemed to float in a silver haze. Soon the sun would make a clear day of it.

Why wait for Grandfather? I thought. *The water can't be that far away. I can already smell the tang of salt air. I'll bet I can find the docks easy enough.*

In no time, I had snuck out of the house without disturbing Grandmother and made my way to the waterfront. I had never imagined there could be so many ships. I walked past about thirty of them—big and small—and there were still ship masts as far as I could see down the Mersey River around which the port of Liverpool was built.

This was great! I couldn't wait until Grandfather

was better and could take me aboard some of the ships to meet the captains.

I stopped beside a small clipper ship. The name *Dumfries* was painted on its bow. The crew seemed about ready to cast off, so I climbed on top of a barrel to watch. Soon the sun broke through the mist, and some people walked down the gangplank. When they reached the dock, they turned and waved to a passenger—a young man who looked only about twenty—who remained standing by the ship's rail. I wondered where he was going . . . the lucky dog.

Suddenly, a ship's officer—I could tell by the fancy way he was dressed—yelled, "Where's the cabin boy? It's time to cast off, and he's nowhere to be seen!" The man came to the rail and looked up and down the dock, then yelled to two sailors below who were ready to release the huge ropes that held the ship secure. "You men! We're short a cabin boy." He jerked his head toward the dock and said, "See to it."

"Aye, aye, sir!"

Just then I noticed that one of the women on the dock was sobbing into her handkerchief. The passenger on deck called down, "Mother, don't cry. Please don't cry. I'll be home before you know it."

I was feeling sorry for the woman when suddenly strong arms grabbed me from behind and pulled me off the barrel. In an instant, I was being carried by the two sailors toward the ship. I'm tall for twelve years of age, and I struggled for all I was worth, but it was no use. I could not break free from their firm grasp. When I felt us bouncing up the gang plank, I began to yell for help.

"Hey, what are you doing to that boy?" someone shouted, but just then something hit me on the head, and everything went dark.

❖ ❖ ❖ ❖

When I woke up—the second time on that fateful Monday—I was not in my grandmother's comfortable guest bed. The place was small and dark and damp, not much bigger than a coal bin. The back of my head hurt, and I felt myself swaying back and forth. It did not take me long to figure out that I was on board the *Dumfries*, on my way out to sea.

"Let me out of here!" I yelled. Again and again I called for help without any results. I tried not to panic, but I was scared to death. Why was I grabbed and taken on board? I know I should have waited for Grandfather to come down to the docks, but I hadn't been doing anything wrong—just sitting on that barrel watching.

Then I remembered the officer yelling that the cabin boy was missing and telling the two sailors to take care of it—and he had nodded toward me! I was really frightened. I didn't want to be a cabin boy—not now, not like this.

I started kicking the rough wall. Maybe I could find a loose board or a door that I could kick open. Again and again I kicked the boards, yelling at the top of my lungs.

Finally, someone opened the door of my small cell, and I found myself staring into the face of an African man. "Well, well, what do we have here?" he said. "A stowaway, eh?"

By now I was furious. "I'm no stowaway! I was forced onto this ship. I'm supposed to be back in Liverpool."

"Ha! A likely story," growled the seaman. "I say you're a stowaway. Get out of there. I'm takin' you to the captain. We'll see what he says."

My heart sank. If the officer I'd seen was the captain, my goose was cooked. But at least I wasn't locked up any more, so I followed along behind my "rescuer." Up on deck, everyone seemed busy adjusting the sails and getting things squared away. The officer who had ordered my capture was yelling orders. But I was relieved to see that land was not far off to the east. *Maybe I can talk him into putting me ashore*, I thought.

However, the sailor passed the officer and took me up some steps to the poop deck where the helmsman was holding the wheel that guided the ship. Beside him stood a large, muscular man. I thought he was just another sailor, plainly dressed in dark blue dungarees, a sweater, and a small-billed cap on his head. He stood there with his arms crossed staring off at the sea, while he puffed evenly on a short pipe.

"Cap'n," said the sailor who had me in tow, "I found this here stowaway up in the forecastle. What'll we do with him?"

I was startled. This was the captain? For the first time, the man with the pipe took notice of us. His face was lean and lined, as though it had been chiseled out of brown ivory. His eyes were a brilliant blue under bushy white eyebrows. He didn't look mean, but he sure looked firm. "What's that, Jeffries? A stowaway? Why in heaven's name, boy, would you want to stow away on a tea clipper bound for China?"

"I didn't stow away," I protested. "I was just sitting on the dock watching. Some of your sailors grabbed me and carried me on board for no reason. They hit me on the head and locked me up below deck."

The captain frowned. "Mr. Henson," he called to the officer in the fancy clothes. "Do you know anything about this boy?"

"Yes, sir," said Henson as he strolled toward the poop deck, the brass buttons on his jacket shining brightly. "That there is our new cabin boy."

"Did you sign him on?"

"Waal, I haven't got 'round to the formalities yet, but I'll do so soon as we get squared away."

"Henson, did you shanghai this kid? I want a straight answer!"

"Yes, sir. That I did. Our signed cabin boy turned up missing when it was time to cast off, and this chap was just sittin' on the dock needin' a job."

"Henson, that is the last time you will shanghai *anyone* onto my ship. Is that understood? You've never sailed with me before, and I can see you have a few things to learn. If you want to remain my first mate, you'd better learn them mighty quick."

"Aye, aye, sir," Henson said with a smirk, and sauntered off again.

I was beginning to get worried. "Can you send me back to Liverpool?" I asked the captain.

The captain shook his head. "Don't see how I can, boy. "Yonder goes our pilot boat. Could have sent you back on it, but it's gone now."

I looked back toward Liverpool where the captain was pointing with the stem of his pipe to see a small boat disappearing in the distance.

Now I was really worried. "Can't you call them back or something?"

"Nope. Besides, the pilot is a busy man; he can't be running a ferry service."

"But my grandfather is a captain! I'm sure he would make it right with the pilot."

"A ship's captain? What's his name?"

"Captain Thompson."

"George Thompson?"

"Yes, sir. He knows everyone. He'll make it right by you if you just get me back to shore."

"I'm sure he would . . ." The captain's voice trailed off as he looked out to sea once more.

I looked around anxiously. "How about putting me on shore with that longboat? It's not that far. I'll—I'll walk back to Liverpool."

The captain frowned. "Look, son, there's no way. Now, I'm sorry you got shanghaied, but like it or not, looks like you're going to be our cabin boy on this voyage. My advice would be to make the most of it. Your granddaddy would be proud of you going to sea." Then he turned to the helmsman and said, "A little to the starboard there. We don't need to crowd the *Sea Witch*."

I turned to see a sharp-looking clipper ship, its sails puffed out like white balloons, heading in the opposite direction off our port bow. Behind it, massive thunderheads climbed high into the blue sky. It was a beautiful picture, but I wasn't interested in pretty pictures at that point.

"Captain, please!" I cried desperately. "Can't you hail that ship and put me aboard back to Liverpool?"

The captain's frown deepened as he glanced up at the wall of clouds. "There's a storm a brewin'," he said, almost as if he were talking to himself, "and I wish we were out of the Irish Channel. It would take a couple hours to make a transfer . . . we don't have that kind of time. But I will do one thing for you." He headed over to the windward side of the ship and picked up a shiny brass speaking trumpet. He put it to his lips and yelled, "Ahoy, the *Sea Witch*!"

In a few moments, the captain of the *Sea Witch* came to the rail of his ship with a similar trumpet. The two ships were almost opposite each other when he called, "Ahoy, Captain Morris! What can we do for you?"

"Tell Captain Thompson in Liverpool that I have his grandson on board as my cabin boy, and all's well!"

"Will do, Captain. Have a good voyage," came the final cry and a friendly wave across the water as the two sleek ships passed each other not more than two hundred feet apart.

"There, young man, now your grandfather won't worry about you."

I was supposed to be grateful? My last chance for getting home was sailing away from us across the leaden water toward Liverpool! I swallowed hard. I was on my way to China without anyone asking me if I wanted to go.

Chapter 2

The Fearsome Light on Holyhead

CAPTAIN MORRIS, taking no further notice of me, stuffed his pipe back in his mouth and turned back to the helmsman.

Fighting back tears, I moved to the back of the ship where I watched the white foam trailing out behind us toward Liverpool. A great sadness swept over me. But just then the wind puffed strongly, and the *Dumfries* heeled far over to its side. I turned around just in time to see the lee rail along the midship dip into the sea. It scared me right out of my homesick blues, and I grabbed some nearby rigging, fearing the ship was about to tip over.

The captain, who was then in front of me, didn't even reach out for anything to steady himself, but moved with the roll of the ship, keeping perfect balance. Soon the ship straightened some, and the captain called out to his first mate, "Mr. Henson! Set the royals and brace the yards. And trim up this spanker, too. I want to make as much headway as possible before that storm hits or we'll be beating right into the teeth of the wind.

"As a matter of fact, Mr. Henson," the captain said as the first mate came up the steps onto the poop deck, "be forewarned. If you don't want to run afoul of me, see that we always carry as much canvas as this ship can handle and that it's trimmed as true as blue. Time is money, Mr. Henson. Time is money. I once made it to Hong Kong in eighty-seven days, and I'd like to match that to Shanghai. Do you understand?"

"Aye, aye, sir!" snapped Henson with a red face, and he turned and started shouting orders to the crew.

At that time, I had no idea what the instructions about the different sails meant, but in moments sailors were climbing up the rigging and pulling on various ropes. I was glad to see it because I figured the ship would soon straighten up and sail so that the deck was level and safe to walk on again. Instead, when the seamen opened the royals—the sails at the very top of the masts—and adjusted the other sails, the ship again tipped over so far that the leeward rail was almost in the water.

When the captain looked around and saw me hanging on for all I was worth, he broke into a big grin and chuckled, "What's the matter, boy? You'll never make a sailor like that. Why don't you go forward and find the cook. Tell him you're the cabin boy and need something to do."

I just stood there hanging on.

"Forward, boy." Then realizing that I didn't know where to find the cook, he pointed to the deckhouse just behind the foremast. "That's the galley. He's in there."

"All right," I managed as I tried to stagger along the steep deck.

"It's not 'all right.' It's 'aye, aye, sir!' "

"Okay, Captain."

"*Sir!*" he thundered.

"Aye, aye, sir," I finally sputtered, fearing I was about to slip into the sea. Actually, the tilt of the deck was not that steep; I've played on house roofs that were much steeper back home, but the deck kept moving with the swells of the sea so that my footing was unsure.

Once down off the poop deck, I made my way forward along the high side of the deck—the windward side—when a curling wave struck the side of the ship and splashed a salt spray on my face. I remembered how wonderful the salty air had smelled just that morning from my grandparents' guest room window. Things had sure changed since then.

The sea was really rolling by this time. The water was as dark as gray slate with lacy patterns of foam stretched over its surface. The clouds that had towered like snow-capped mountains when I had first seen them were now upon us, hanging low, their dark bellies almost dragging across the crests of the waves.

The *Dumfries* had three tall masts. The forward two were fitted with four square sails each; three jib sails flew out to the front of the foremast. The mizzenmast (the mast at the back of the ship) had a large boom on it with what I later learned were the spanker and the gaff sails. Between the masts were stretched various staysails. It was a handsome ship of about 120 feet in length, though not nearly so large or fast as some of the newer ships.

When I finally reached the galley, it was so small that I couldn't imagine anyone preparing a meal for fifty men in it. But there was the cook, a short, pudgy man in a greasy shirt, stirring a huge pot on top of a big, black iron stove.

"Sir," I said, "the captain sent me."

" 'Sir,' am I?" the cook said without turning around. "Since when have I been promoted to an officer? And who might you be?"

"I'm Neil Thompson, and I don't belong here."

"Then get out," he growled.

"I mean," I corrected myself, "I don't *really* belong on this ship, but since I'm here, I'm supposed to be the cabin boy."

He squinted at me then. "Shanghaied, eh? In that case, you better get to work. There's a sack of potatoes. There's a knife. Start peeling."

I found a crate to sit on and started in on the spuds. I hadn't realized that peeling potatoes was such hard work! But the cook didn't speak to me again until I'd finished.

The forward deckhouse, known as the forecastle, contained the galley and the crew's bunk rooms. It had portholes along the sides, just like the window in my bedroom at my grandparents' house. But it was getting so dark outside that the cook lit two brass lanterns swinging from the beams overhead. Their light cast strange dancing shadows around the small room, which, along with the constant creaking and groaning of the ship's timbers and bulkheads, reminded me that the weather outside was not getting any calmer.

Sometimes a wave would splash against the portholes, and my imagination went back and forth between hoping the storm would get so bad that the captain would have to turn back for Liverpool, to fearing that we were surely going to sink.

When I finished peeling the potatoes, the cook said, "Put the peels in that bucket and throw them overboard. When you get back, you can start cleaning up these pots."

As I came out onto the deck, I heard someone yell, "Here she comes!" I had no idea what *she* was, but in the dim light I saw the first mate, Henson, leaping like a madman for the main rigging, climbing frantically until he was several feet above the deck.

Then I saw it: A great wave, curling and foaming, was poised high above the rail, and I was directly under it!

"Grab hold of something, boy, or you'll wash overboard!" Henson shouted at me. I should have sprung

for the rigging, but being new to the ways of the sea, my mind did not work quickly enough. Before I could move, the descending wall of water knocked me down and sent me skidding across the deck. Buried under water, I was certain I had been washed into the raging sea, until I crashed into something. Then I was rolled over and over like a bowling ball among tenpins. I figured I must be against the leeward rail and tried desperately to grab hold of something but with no luck.

Then suddenly, almost as quickly as it had struck, the flood subsided as the water drained away, and I was able to breathe again.

I stood up trembling and saw that I had been rolled the full length of the midship deck and had come to rest against the steps going up to the poop deck. From above, the captain yelled down to me, "Better grab that bucket. We don't have any extras."

I couldn't believe it! I had almost been washed overboard, and all he could say was "grab that bucket"? However, in the next few days I learned that getting knocked off your feet in heavy weather was so common to a sailor that if you came up safe, there was nothing more to worry about.

I grabbed the bucket that was still rolling around on the deck and headed back to the galley as fast as I could go on the plunging deck. When I had slammed the door behind me to keep out the storm, the cook turned and said, "If you're gonna stand there dripping like Friday's laundry, you might as well wring yourself out into that pot so you can start washin' it."

It was long after dark and the storm was still howling when the crew finished eating in shifts. By the time I finished scrubbing the supper pots, I was so tired that I found a warm, dry spot near the stove and curled up to sleep.

✧ ✧ ✧ ✧

In spite of the roll of the ship, I must have slept most of night away because there was a gray tinge to the portholes when I awoke as someone nudged me with his boot. It was the black sailor again. "You awake, Thompson?" the man asked. Then, not waiting for an answer, he said, "Get up, and come with me. Water's leaking through the main hatch into the hold."

He led me to a little companionway where steps led down to the next deck. There, he lit a smoky candle and looked me in the eye. "My name's Jeffries; I'm the ship's steward," he said, then he moved forward to where a waterfall streamed through a hatch from the deck above and disappeared into the main hold below us.

"Hold this," the steward said as he handed me the candle and climbed up to adjust the hatch so it fit properly. Immediately the surging cascade of water slowed to a thin curtain and then a trickle.

"You'll be bunking aft with me and workin' for me most of the time," Jeffries grunted. "But right now all hands are needed on deck. First we better get you into an oilskin."

He got me a raincoat that had been oiled to make it waterproof, and we headed out on the deck. "You can help with the pumps," he shouted over the wind. "That don't take no skill."

Topside, it was almost impossible to breathe as the fierce gusts seemed to suck the air right out of my lungs. I followed Jeffries to two large wheels near the base of the mainmast. There was a large handle on each wheel and two sailors were cranking away. I relieved one sailor and Jeffries relieved the other.

At first it didn't seem too hard to turn the wheels, and I was glad to have something to hang on to and someone nearby in the middle of the storm. But it wasn't long until I was breathing hard.

Sometimes several waves thundered down onto our deck one right after the other, filling it full to the bulwarks with sea water, but I held on until the flood subsided.

All the other sailors were on deck, too, working hard to obey the first mate's orders, but it was difficult to hear them with the roar of the wind whistling through the rigging. Every few minutes he would shout: "Ready to come about," and the men would run for different lines.

Then the ship would turn into the wind while the sailors scrambled to adjust the sails. When the sails began to fill, the ship heeled over in the other direction, and the mate called, "Let go and haul!"

Back and forth we tacked into the teeth of the wind all morning, and I could see that the sailors were exhausted. Once Jeffries yelled above the wind, "I don't think we're making any headway!"

Only one square sail was set per mast along with the storm staysails and the two jib sails. The wind was so strong that all the rest had been taken down during the night so that the masts wouldn't break. Finally, a new order came: "Stand by to heave her to!" Then a moment later, "Port! Hard a port! Reef the topsails!"

A dozen men scampered up the main rigging and worked their way out on the spars to take down the sails.

"What are they doing?" I yelled in Jeffries' ear, fearing that the men would surely fall to their death on the deck or into the foaming sea.

"They're taking down the sails because we aren't making any headway. Maybe we can ride it out for a while. At least it will give the sailors a bit of a break."

A sea anchor was thrown out, and the ship began to bob and sway in an entirely new manner. Within moments I was seasick. I threw up before I could get to the rail, but the mess was immediately washed away as a wave came crashing across the deck. After that I had the dry heaves, not having eaten anything since the night before.

I made the mistake of looking out to sea and saw a great wave of liquid green with its milk-white crest rising so high that it became a mountain hiding the rest of the throbbing ocean from view. Higher and higher, thinner and thinner its crest grew as it began to curl, ready to break, until with a roar it fell over the ship, sending the sailors sprawling in all directions. Jeffries saw it, too, and we both stopped pumping and entwined our arms in the pump wheels to keep from being washed away.

When the deck had drained, I was suddenly joined at the pump wheel by the passenger I had seen by the rail the day before. The young man took hold of the wheel and gave me a hand with the pumping.

"I'm Hudson Taylor," he shouted. His fair hair was plastered on his forehead by the driving rain.

"Neil Thompson," I gasped above the scream of the gale.

At that moment, the ship rose on a swell nearly as large as the wave that had just crashed over us, and I could see a light not far off our port stern. It shone clearly against the dark gray horizon where the sea and sky merged together. "Look! A light! A light!" I screamed. It was a welcome sight to me; I thought it meant friendship, help, maybe even warmth and cover from the storm. But one look at the light and Jeffries' face turned to horror.

"Land, ho!" went up the call over the howl of the wind, and it was repeated up and down the deck. I saw the captain examining the light with his spyglass, then he thundered, "Get some sail up, Mr. Henson! That's Holyhead, and we'll wreck on its rocks for sure!" The beam from Holyhead that should have been a comforting sight had become a fearsome light.

"If either of you landlubbers knows how to pray, now's the time!" shouted Jeffries to Mr. Taylor and me, his eyes wide with fear.

Chapter 3

High Above the Sea

To my surprise, Hudson Taylor started right in praying while cranking the pump wheel. "Oh, Father," he prayed aloud, "have mercy on your children! See us in danger here on this sea. Save us from being dashed on those rocks—"

Jeffries also was mumbling frantically, punctuated with "Lord!" and "Save us!"

I didn't know what to do, so I tried to say the Lord's Prayer. I hadn't gone to church much—though my mother was always saying we ought to go more often—so I couldn't remember it all. But when I got to the "Amen," Jeffries and Hudson Taylor were still praying and cranking, cranking and praying. I was surprised that they weren't reciting some memorized prayers, which was the only thing I had heard the priest say in church. They were talking to God like He was standing right there.

Finally, Hudson Taylor stopped and leaned toward the steward. "I really don't think we have anything to worry about, brother," he shouted. He had a smile on his handsome face, with his long straight nose and hint of a curly, red beard on his chin.

"What do you mean?" asked Jeffries, still wild-eyed.

"God has called me to be a missionary to China," Taylor shouted above the wind, "and He put me on this ship to get me there. So I'm sure we'll make it safely."

"Captain Morris would be glad to hear that," returned Jeffries, but a smile cracked his anxious face.

By this time, as much sail was set as the *Dumfries* could tolerate in such a gale, and the ship once again tacked back and forth, trying to gain a little headway into the wind with each leg of the tack. After about ten minutes on the starboard tack, Henson gave the orders for the ship to come about, and we did ten minutes on the port tack. The seamen barely had time to catch their breath after getting the sails trimmed before they had to do it again. But when I looked back toward the light, we had not made any headway. In fact, I could now see that the light was coming from a lighthouse sitting on a rugged point of land.

All afternoon the battle with the storm continued. Sometimes the light from Holyhead seemed dimmer and farther away; then I would look back a few minutes later and realize that it had dimmed only because fog or a small rain squall had obscured the lighthouse.

The three of us worked on the pumps as hard as we could, taking short breaks when we were too exhausted to continue. Once when we were resting, Captain Morris came by. I thought he was going to scold us for not pumping, but instead he said, "Mr. Taylor! I appreciate your lending a hand. We need everyone's help in a storm like this."

"Glad to help," said the ship's passenger. "But I'm not too worried." Then he told the captain about God wanting him to go to China.

"That is some comfort," said the captain. "But don't forget what happened when the Apostle Paul sailed for Rome."

"What do you mean?"

"As I remember the Bible story, even though everyone on the ship survived, the ship wrecked on the island of Malta. I would most sincerely like to save my ship." The captain tipped his small-billed cap. "So I thank you for your prayers and for helping with the pumps."

The storm raged on, but as evening approached, the sun broke through momentarily in the western sky. The brilliance of it seemed to give everyone a surge of hope, but it also showed up the fury of the storm. Suddenly the sky and sea and clouds changed from murky shades of gray to stark black and white with highlights of gold around the edges of the clouds. Out of the western clouds bright sunbeams angled down to the sea, shining crystal-green through the tops of the waves.

I looked back toward the lighthouse and saw for the first time how treacherous the coast was. There was no beach, only huge black rocks onto which the waves were beating with ceaseless fury, casting spray and foam as high as the base of the lighthouse.

For a moment the sun shown on the lighthouse standing like a solitary white pillar against the slate-black clouds. At the top beamed the warning beacon. There was no question in my mind. If we were driven against those sharp rocks, the ship would be crushed, and, in spite of what Mr. Taylor had said, *I* couldn't imagine any of us surviving such a wreck.

With each tack that the ship took back and forth we were losing ground, driven by the wind and waves closer and closer to that awful coast. The sun was setting, and suddenly the sky began to turn gold, then orange, then red.

Jeffries looked up with an expression of relief on his face. " 'Red sky at night, sailor's delight; red sky in the morning, sailor's warning,' " he muttered, reciting the old sailors' proverb. "If we can hang on, this storm might be blowing itself out. Lord knows, it's blown long enough for three storms."

The angry sea looked like hell itself as it turned red and black, reflecting the eerie colors of the sky. We were on our port tack and coming closer and closer to Holyhead when the first mate finally gave the order, "Ready to come about!"

"No, Mr. Henson!" shouted Captain Morris from the poop deck. "Steady as she goes!"

"Captain," protested the first mate, "if we get any closer, we could be caught in the currents and pushed right into the rocks when we try to come about."

"I know that, Henson. Steady, lads. Steady as she goes."

"But Captain—"

"Mr. Henson, I will not have my orders questioned. Stow it, or get below!" The captain turned back to the helmsman. "Two degrees to the port, sailor."

The ship responded immediately and picked up a little more wind, but turning to the port meant we were turning toward the rocky point. Jeffries and Taylor and I stopped cranking the pumps and just held on for dear life.

"He's going to try and run it," said the steward through clinched teeth. "I don't see how we can make it."

Then I, too, could see what the captain was doing. Instead of coming about and heading away from the point on another tack, hoping to work his way out away from the coast a little farther—which hadn't been succeeding all day—he was going to try and shoot past the point of land.

The point was getting closer and closer. Even above the wind, we could hear the waves crashing on the rocks and see the spray flying high into the air and up onto the shore.

"Hold her steady, now. This is our only chance, lads," encouraged the captain. "One more point to the port, helmsman."

Oh, no, I thought. *We can't get any closer!* We were no more than two ship lengths off the rocks, and were still being thrashed around by violent waves. But then I saw that we might have a chance. The ship came even with the lighthouse and slowly, very slowly, moved past it. Then we were even with the outermost rocks and moving past them.

Suddenly, a great cheer went up from the crew. "We made it! We made it!" And sure enough, the stern of the ship had passed Holyhead.

Not far beyond the point, the wind and the currents changed somewhat; and Captain Morris told the helmsman to bring the ship around several points to the starboard where, for the first time since the storm hit, we began making headway away from the coast and toward the southwest.

"I'll see you in my cabin, Mr. Henson, if you please," growled the captain, turning control of the ship over to the second mate.

Scowling, the first mate followed the captain below deck. I wondered why he looked so unhappy. We were all safe from the storm—including Mr. Henson. Shouldn't that make him glad? Of course, Captain Morris had shown his seamanship and courage to be superior to the first mate's. *Guess that's why the captain is the captain,* I thought.

"It's hard for a proud man like the first mate to 'eat crow' in front of the whole crew," murmured Hudson Taylor in my ear. It was like he'd read my mind.

✧ ✧ ✧ ✧

In the weeks that followed, I learned what "normal" life aboard ship was like. We had good winds and pleasant weather with only occasional rain squalls—nothing like the storm we'd survived in the Irish Channel.

As cabin boy, my duties were to assist the steward, whom I liked, and the cook, who was a sour old man. I was given a "berth" (a narrow wooden bunk) in the steward's cabin that was below the poop deck along with the cabins for the ship's officers, the captain, and any passengers. I cleaned the officers' bathroom, made up the captain's and the passenger's beds each day, and helped Mr. Jeffries clean up the dishes after the officers and Mr. Taylor ate in the dining saloon. Hudson Taylor was the only passenger on ship, and he wasn't a finicky sort of person, so I didn't have to spend a lot of time serving him.

In the galley, I was stuck with the most boring jobs—like peeling potatoes and washing pots again and again. There always seemed to be some greasy pot to scrub.

Even when the regular tasks were done, there were brass lanterns or the captain's boots that needing polishing. "Idle hands are the devil's tools," Jeffries warned me a dozen times. "At sea, it's good for everyone to keep busy." But I could see that he wasn't just picking on me. The mates kept all the sailors busy. If the winds were steady and the sailors weren't needed to constantly adjust the sails, they were put to work scrubbing the deck or climbing up in the rigging to tar and repair the ropes. Any hand who was caught loafing was quickly "encouraged" back to work by the kicks and curses of the first and second mates.

It seemed like bells were always bonging. I soon learned that a twenty-four-hour day at sea was divided into six segments of four hours each. During each segment, a bell rang on the half hours—once after the first half hour, twice after the second, and so on, until the end of that segment was announced with eight bells. The segment from four P.M. to eight P.M. was divided in half (the "first dogwatch" and the "second dogwatch") to allow everyone to eat supper.

The crew was also divided into two teams. One team, called the "port watch," served under the first mate. The other, serving under the second mate, was the "starboard watch." When the weather was good, the "watches" took turns sailing the ship—four hours on and four hours off, except for the afternoon and evening watches when each had one of the dog-watches attached, making them six hours in length.

When the weather was bad, the call went out, "All hands on deck!" and everyone helped until the storm subsided or until the sails were "reefed" enough (tied part-way up) to ride out the storm. Seeing the sailors high above the deck, clinging to the rigging as they tried to reef a sail in a strong wind, made me nervous. I half expected someone to slip and fall to his death below.

Then one day Captain Morris said to me, "Thompson, how about you going up in the boatswain's chair and tarring some ropes today? Any landlubber can scrub pots or polish brass. Your grandfather would keelhaul me if I took you all the way to China without teaching you any seamanship. Jeffries, set him up."

My mouth went dry. The boatswain's "chair" looked like my childhood tree swing—except its rope went high into the rigging of the ship through a pulley near the spars. I looked up at the towering masts. Even though the weather was fair with a light breeze and a low sea, the masts were swaying back and forth. I was so scared that I paid very little attention as Jeffries brought out an old canvas shirt with smears of tar all over it. Then he handed me a little pot of tar with a stiff brush in it.

"When you get up there, tie this safety line around the rigging you are working on," the steward said, tying a length of rope securely to my pants belt. "It'll keep you from swinging so much and let you use both hands to work. And whatever you do, don't let any tar drip onto the deck below, or you'll be licking it off all night."

Before I knew what was happening, I was being lifted high above the deck in the chair. "Don't look down!" Jeffries yelled. I hung on for dear life as the sailors pulled me higher and higher. When I was near the top of the mast, Jeffries started calling out instructions. "Start with that backstay rope right there by your right hand. . . . No, not that one. It's already been done. The aft one."

I was clinging to the ropes of my boatswain's chair with both hands and had no intention of letting go to grab the piece of rigging he was talking about. But my hands were aching, and I was slowly turning around and around in the wind. I had to make my spinning stop. Finally, I reached out with one foot and almost caught the rope I was supposed to tar. The next time I came around, I used both feet and got it.

I pulled myself to the rigging and clung there with my legs wrapped around the rope. "That's right!

That's right!" encouraged Jeffries. He sounded a mile below me, and the wind seemed much stronger up there. "Now tie your safety line to the stay, then you can work."

If he thought I was going to let go, he was crazy! But after I'd hung in the air ten minutes or so, I realized that the only way down was to work my way down. I had to do something. But two bells rang before I got my safety line tied. Finally, I felt secure enough to let go with one hand and reach for the little brush in the tar pot that was attached to the chair.

I dabbed a little tar on the stay above my hand and then some more, rubbing it into the

rope on all sides to protect it from the rain and weather. Soon I had a two-foot section finished—as far as I could reach from that position.

"Ready to move?" called Jeffries before I had a chance to rest.

"Yeah." He lowered me until I said, "Hold."

When three bells rang, I was ready to move again. Then I made the mistake of looking down. From the deck it had seemed like the ship was riding almost level, but up in the rigging I found that it was heeled over enough so that I was actually out over the sea. I jammed the brush in the pot and some tar splashed out as I grabbed for the stay.

"Hey, what the—?" someone yelled from below, then I heard cursing and screaming. "Do I work in a barn now? Do I have to look out for chickens roosting over my head?" I looked down again. Somehow the wind had blown the blob of tar back over the deck where it landed on the sailmaker's bald head.

The angry sailmaker pulled out his knife and reached toward the rope that raised and lowered my boatswain's chair. "I'm gonna cut you down and feed you to the sharks," he yelled.

I was plenty scared, but I didn't think he'd actually do it until I saw Mr. Taylor run across the deck. He grabbed the sailmaker's arm and stood between the angry man's knife and the rope. Then he said something to the man that I couldn't understand. "Okay, okay," said the sailmaker. "But if it happens again, he goes in the drink. You hear me?"

The man stomped away, cursing as he went. "I

told you to be careful with that tar," Jeffries called up, grinning.

When the steward finally lowered me to the deck, Mr. Taylor sauntered up to me and clapped me on the back. "Brave lad," he said, his blue-gray eyes twinkling. I wanted to thank him for coming to my rescue, but my tongue seemed stuck in my throat. I didn't feel very brave.

For the next several days the captain sent me back up in the boatswain's chair until finally I lost my fear of hanging up there between the sky and the sea. I even started to enjoy swaying back and forth in the rigging.

The ship turned east away from the coast of South America and headed for the Cape of Good Hope around the bottom of Africa. From up in the rigging I could see for miles as we sailed on day after day, and I was the first to sight two other ships off on the horizon. But the view I enjoyed most were the dolphins bounding along before our ship. They kept us company for mile after mile, then they disappeared for hours or days until, suddenly, they would show up again. Some of the sailors said they were just different schools of dolphins, but I felt sure I recognized some of them. It was comforting to think that the same dolphins returned again and again to guide us.

Chapter 4

Overboard

ONCE WE ROUNDED THE CAPE OF GOOD HOPE at the bottom of Africa we had good sailing through the South Indian Ocean. We sailed to within 120 miles of Australia, but in February, as we passed through the islands of Indonesia, there were whole days when we sat becalmed. The sails hung limp or flapped uselessly from time to time, and we drifted on a hot and glassy sea.

Fortunately, at night a breeze usually came up that allowed modest headway, but a southwesterly current flowed through the islands and drove us back during many of the windless days.

It was during this time, when there were idle hours on deck (you can't swab the deck all day every day), that I got to know the ship's passenger better.

Hudson Taylor had asked permission to have Sunday worship services on deck. Captain Morris, Jeffries, the African steward, and the ship's carpenter enthusiastically supported these services and attended whenever  the weather allowed.

I attended the worship services, too, because I liked Hudson Taylor and Jeffries and the captain. But very few of the other sailors participated. If they happened to be on deck, a few sometimes stood around and listened out of boredom. But if they were sleeping or playing checkers or anything else, they didn't trouble themselves in the least to "go to church" even when Jeffries or Taylor invited them.

That surprised me. I was taught that England was a Christian country, so I thought most of those English sailors would be Christians. But living together so closely on the ship, I began to see a difference between people. A few men, of course, scoffed at any belief in God. I expected that, and it didn't surprise me. But most of the men just didn't care . . . even though they had been born and baptized in the church, some married in the church, and most would probably have their funerals in it. They called themselves Christian, but most of them had no real desire to "take up their cross and follow Jesus"—as Mr. Taylor put it.

That started me thinking. If I had to tell the truth, I was that kind of a "Christian," too. Feeling somewhat guilty, I faithfully attended every service Mr. Taylor held on deck.

One day Hudson Taylor preached on the third commandment: "Thou shalt not take the name of the Lord thy God in vain." I had never thought about what it meant to use God's name in vain. The sailors on the *Dumfries* were a foul-talking bunch, and I knew it was wrong to use some of the bad words they said. But Taylor explained that to say "Oh, God" or call out to "Jesus Christ" for help could be short prayers if you were seriously speaking to God. But if you were not really speaking to God, then it was using His name in vain.

When I thought about it, I could see that when most of the sailors said those words, they weren't speaking *to* God; they just used His name to express surprise, disgust, or anger. For the first time I understood the commandment and decided to be more careful about the way I talked. I wasn't sure what it meant to be a Christian like Mr. Taylor and Captain Morris, but there wasn't any reason to be rude to God. After all, someday I might really need Him!

One still, hot Sunday morning the ocean currents had taken us dangerously near the north shore of New Guinea. During Mr. Taylor's worship service, I noticed that Captain Morris looked worried and frequently left our little circle to look over the side of the ship. Taylor noticed it, too, and after his closing prayer said, "What's the problem, Captain? You seem troubled."

"That I am, Mr. Taylor. The current is very swift through here and not far out there are a line of reefs. Without a breeze, we will soon be on them, and a sharp coral reef can put a hole in the side of a ship as sure as those rocks of Holyhead."

The captain turned and shouted for a man to go up in the rigging with a spyglass to watch for the reefs. Another hour passed without wind, when the man aloft called out, "There they are! About a quarter mile astern."

Everyone ran to the rail to get a look, but we couldn't see anything. In about ten minutes, Captain Morris asked the lookout if we were getting closer.

"No question about it, sir. You ought to be able to see them yourself by now."

I looked where he was pointing and thought I could see a light green streak in the water where the swells were flatter.

"Mr. Henson," the captain said to the first mate, "launch the longboat and put every hand in it who can pull an oar. Maybe we can tow the *Dumfries* away from harm."

The longboat, with two men per oar, tugged at us for an hour. It may have slowed our approach to the reef, but I could still see we were losing ground. The line of the reef in the water was now very distinct— and no more than a hundred yards away.

Suddenly, moving along the green line of the reef, I saw a gray shadow. I blinked, thinking the glare from the sun was bothering my eyes. But just then the man aloft sang out, "Sharks! Sharks!"

The prospect of wrecking on a reef in calm water had not seemed to upset the crew much, but the addition of sharks changed everything. Panic seemed to spread throughout the ship. Some of the men started untying the lifeboats. "Until I give the order to abandon ship, those boats stay where they are," roared the captain. "Touch them again, and you'll go below deck."

I stared at the gray shapes. The sharks were fifteen to eighteen feet long. Occasionally, a triangular fin would break the water, sending a shiver down my spine.

Captain Morris called back the longboat and turned to Hudson Taylor. "We'll need the longboat along with all the lifeboats if any of us are to live through this. We have done everything that can be done. Now, we can only wait. I hope that by some means you still reach China."

"We haven't tried everything," said Taylor.

"No?" The captain raised his bushy eyebrows. "And what might be left to try?"

"There are at least four of us on board who are Christians," said Taylor calmly. "Let's each go to our cabins and agree in prayer to ask the Lord to send us a breeze. He can as easily send it now as at sunset."

The captain rubbed his chin. "Agreed," he said and went off to find the steward and the carpenter. I didn't like being left out, but their actions made clear to me what I had already begun to realize: I hadn't decided *not* to be a Christian, but I had never actually decided to follow Christ, either.

The first mate frowned as he saw the captain and the others disappear below deck. Then he turned back to stare at the sharks in the water. I counted three of them patrolling back and forth along the coral reef, just like they knew we were coming and were waiting to make us their next meal. Back and forth, back and forth. . . .

Suddenly, Hudson Taylor's voice spoke behind us. "Mr. Henson, I think you better let down the corners of the mainsails so we can catch the wind."

"What would be the good of that?" snorted the

first mate.

"Because we've been praying, man, and I'm sure God will send a breeze immediately. But we must be ready."

Henson looked up skeptically at the sails. I looked, too, and thought that the topmost sails—the royals, as they call them—began to tremble.

"Don't you see? The wind is coming!" said Taylor. "Look at the royals!"

"It's only a cat's-paw," scoffed the mate, referring to the little puffs of wind that played at the sails like a cat's paw even on the calmest day.

"Cat's-paw or not," cried Taylor, "let down the sails, man, or we'll be on the reef."

The mate got a very surprised look on his face and gave the order. No sooner were the sails dropped than they snapped full of wind. With a welcome creaking of the ship's timbers the *Dumfries* stopped its backward drifting and slowly started to move forward.

"Thank God!" called Captain Morris as he came running up on deck from his cabin. To everyone's amazement, the breeze held steady until we had passed the Palau Islands and were well away from any dangerous reefs.

✧ ✧ ✧ ✧

On Wednesday, March 1, 1854, we finally dropped anchor in the Port of Shanghai, China, and I was eager to go ashore. We'd been on ship for five and a half months.

Young Mr. Taylor appeared on deck with his various bags and boxes, looking eagerly around at the crowded harbor and the even more crowded shoreline. He made a point to shake hands with the whole crew and thank them for the journey. I knew some of them thought he was a bit odd, but most of them had come to respect the fledgling missionary.

When Taylor came to me I joked, "Don't say goodbye; I'll see you in Shanghai!"

But I hadn't counted on the captain being a spoil sport. "Sorry, Thompson," Captain Morris interrupted. "Shanghai's a terribly wicked city—no place for a young boy to be running around. You are to remain on board ship. There's plenty of work for you to do here." Then he turned to assist Hudson Taylor down the rope ladder into the longboat that would row him to shore.

Anger boiled up inside me. I had been shanghaied at sea twenty-three weeks, and I longed for solid ground under my feet. I knew no one was supposed to argue with the captain, but I couldn't help it. As the longboat pulled away from the *Dumfries*, I pulled at the captain's sleeve. "I was kidnapped and brought aboard this ship against my will!" I protested. "The least you can do is give me my liberty now that we're in port."

Captain Morris's eyes narrowed and his face got stern. "I said, remain aboard, and that's what I meant." He turned and stalked away.

I couldn't believe it! Not go ashore? Once again I

felt like a prisoner.

Sitting at anchor in the Port of Shanghai—which was nothing more than a wide bend in the dirty Whangpoo River—was a lot worse than being at sea. The monotony of remaining on board—sometimes almost alone, except for a watch of two or three sailors—made me more homesick than ever.

Jeffries and the cook did their best to keep me busy, but I had lots of time to stare at the exotic world just beyond my reach. Dozens of other ships rode at anchor—even some British warships, and between us weaved the ever-present Chinese "junks" trying to sell hot rice and vegetables, strange-looking fruit, and rolls of cloth to the foreign sailors. I watched as barges were towed alongside the big ships to load them with tea and other goods to sell back in England or America.

Endless days passed, but no barge pulled alongside the *Dumfries*. "Where's our load of tea?" I asked Jeffries one night when he came back aboard ship.

"We may not get any tea," he frowned.

"Why not?"

"There's a war starting in Shanghai."

"A war? Who with? I don't see the British warships doing anything."

Jeffries looked disgusted. "It's not that kind of war. It's a Chinese thing. A bunch of rebels called the Red Turbans are trying to take over the Chinese part of the city. They're not bothering the European settlements or you *would* see those men-o'-war moving against them."

"But what's that got to do with our tea?"

"I guess the fighting has upset the Chinese trade routes, so tea growers can't ship as much tea down the river. Less tea, higher prices for what's available, and right now, the price is so high that the company couldn't make any money. So, here we sit. Maybe it'll get better in a couple of days."

I felt like hitting something . . . or someone. It wasn't fair! I wanted to get home, but here we were stuck in China, and I wasn't even permitted to leave ship. More days passed, and still there was no tea.

Then one morning Jeffries told me we would be loading our cargo the next day—but it wasn't going to be tea. "Aiken & Company owns the *Dumfries*," he said, "and they have offices here in Shanghai. The agent has arranged for us to take a load of silk and other supplies to San Francisco. I guess those Californians have struck it rich with their gold rush, and now they want to dress in style." He snorted sarcastically. "Maybe when we get back to Shanghai in six months or so the price of tea will be down to where Aiken can make a profit on it. Who knows? But that's the way it goes with the shipping business."

I nearly collapsed in a cold sweat. Three months to America and three months back to China! Then, *if everything went well,* another five or six months back to England. And it could be longer! I couldn't wait. That was two years! I'd be fourteen before I got home. My life was being stolen from me all because an impatient first mate hadn't been able to find his cabin boy at sailing time.

As I thought about it, I got angry at the captain, too. He wouldn't take me back to Liverpool when he found I'd been shanghaied, or even stop long enough to put me aboard the *Sea Witch*.

But thinking about the *Sea Witch* gave me an idea. The harbor was full of other ships. One of them had to be going directly back to England. *What if I jumped ship and got passage on another clipper?* I thought. But I had no money. *Then why not sign on as crew?* It might work, but that was a dangerous thing to do. I'd heard plenty of horror stories of mean captains who flogged their crew at sea. I had to admit that life on board the *Dumfries* hadn't been too bad.

But two years? I couldn't wait that long! I decided to take my chances and jump ship at the first opportunity.

My break came just after three bells in the first dogwatch. The only man on duty went into the galley to find something to eat. I was at the starboard rail when a Chinese junk sailed so close to us I might have jumped on board. Instead, I scrambled over the rail, waited till it had sailed past, then let go, dropping quietly into the water. With a few strong strokes, I swam up behind the junk and grabbed on to a rope trailing in the dirty water.

I hung on and was towed away from the *Dumfries* to the City of Shanghai . . . and a very uncertain future.

Chapter 5

"We Just Shoot You! No Torture"

THE CHINESE JUNK that towed me through the muddy waters of Port of Shanghai did not, of course, dock at the European part of the city but in the Chinese sector. I drifted away from the back of the little boat with its brown fan-like sails and swam to the garbage-strewn bank under some shops that hung out over the river on stilts.

When I crawled out, dripping and smelly, I must have looked like some mud monster rising from the swamp. I made my way between the waterfront shops into a narrow winding street and turned north, hoping to find the European part of the city. The street was full of people; to my surprise they took no notice of me, but I sure took notice of them. Everything was so different!

Long black pigtails hung down everyone's back. Everyone was wearing a long, loose shirt over baggy pants. Some pulled two-wheel carts piled high with items, while others had a pole over their shoulders with baskets of food or buckets of water hanging from the ends.

After a while, I noticed something unusual. In all the hustle and bustle, there were no women in the street. Then I saw a woman and a girl about my age working in some kind of a market booth. But the first thing I noticed about them were the tiny shuffling steps they took when they walked. I stopped and could see why; they both had baby feet, tiny little feet in black shoes. It was the strangest thing— probably an inherited birth defect, I imagined.

The shops and buildings seemed very flimsy. Some were made out of strips of bamboo woven together; others seemed to be covered with a colored paper through which light shone from inside.

I pushed my way through the busy crowd and passed buildings that were more substantial. They had tiled roofs with the corners turned up. When I looked closely in the dim evening light, I could see a carved dragon on the end of each up-turned tip that made them look very scary.

And then I saw another woman walking with the same shuffling little steps. Her feet were very tiny as well. *This is very strange,* I thought.

Exotic smells and "plinky" enchanting music floated through the smoky air as evening meals were prepared over charcoal fires. I realized I was hungry, but I hurried on in search of the European part of town.

The farther north I walked, the streets suddenly seemed to be deserted. The few people I saw darted from building to building after searching the street and looking up at the darkening sky. Nervously, I began to walk faster. As I passed a stone wall, two strong men grabbed me and pulled me into a narrow alley. They pushed me up against the wall and began yelling at me in Chinese. I shook my head and cried, "I don't understand; I don't understand." I tried to pull away and escape, but they slammed me up against the wall so hard that it knocked the breath out of me.

From somewhere another man appeared. He was dressed in a military uniform with a fancy sword hanging from his side. With a wave of his hands, he motioned the two thugs to back off. I breathed with relief as he stood in front of me, his hands on his hips and a cold scowl on his face. "You spy!" he said with a jerk of his goatee at me.

"No, no. I'm just a sailor, a British sailor, a cabin boy."

"You spy!" he said again in English. It wasn't a question. It was a statement. No, it was more like a verdict from a judge. "You spy for Red Turbans." With a silent gesture, he commanded the two thugs to grab me again.

"No, wait! I'm a cabin boy, I tell you—on the ship *Dumfries*. It's right out in the harbor. I can show you." The men grabbed each of my arms and marched

me along behind the officer. "You got it wrong. How could I be a spy?"

"See! You confess. You say, 'I be a spy.' You confess. That good. We just shoot you! No torture," said the officer over his shoulder.

"No, no, no!" I protested, struggling to break free. He had misunderstood! But the harder I struggled, the tighter the thugs held me and the faster we walked.

Then suddenly there was a whistling sound in the air, followed by a tremendous explosion in the house beside us. The blast knocked us all to the ground. Dazed, I looked around and saw that the man between me and the explosion was seriously wounded by flying debris. His body had shielded me from injury.

Another whistle overhead and the street half a block behind us exploded. Then I heard gunfire from somewhere ahead.

In the commotion, I realized no one was holding me. I jumped to my feet and began running back the way we had come. I turned at the first corner and then at the next, but there, just ahead of me, was a group of soldiers around a cannon set up in the street. A tremendous explosion erupted as the cannon fired right over my head. The blast left my ears ringing. I staggered back a few steps, then turned and ran the other way.

I ran and ran until I turned into another street where the people were walking freely. I could still hear the booms of the cannons and the tat-tat-tat of rifle fire in the distance. But I was lost. *Be calm, be calm*, I told myself. I figured the shooting couldn't be coming from the harbor or from the north, because that was the European sector. So the fighting had to be either west or south. I guessed west, and started walking in the direction I thought was north.

The streets in the Chinese section of Shanghai did not run straight, however, so when the shooting stopped for a few minutes, I had to be careful. After two or three turns, I was uncertain again which way was north.

Finally, I crossed a bridge over a canal or river and came into what was obviously the European sector. I was as surprised at what I found there as I had been in the Chinese city. I had expected only a few rough wooden buildings thrown up as a sort of government fort or outpost. Instead, I came upon stately brick houses with splendid gardens, two tall churches, and several large government buildings, three and four stories high.

It was night, but the lights from the buildings and the streetlamps gave a soft glow to the bustling community. There were very few horse-drawn carriages on the streets, but the local citizens got around just as fast—if not faster—by riding in fancy sedan chairs carried by fast-stepping Chinese coolies.

Sailors, many of them loud and partially drunk, strolled in small groups from tavern to tavern.

It felt good to be in somewhat familiar surroundings again, but I realized that I had no place to stay and no money for food. The government buildings and branch offices for the various shipping lines were all closed, so there was no chance that night to find a job on a ship back to London.

I was looking in the door of a tavern, trying to think of some way to get something to eat, when I heard voices behind me. "Hey, there's our cabin boy, Thompson," one said.

I turned around. The sailors were from the *Dumfries*, and right in the middle was Henson, the first mate. "What are you doing here?" he challenged. "I thought the captain told you to stay aboard ship."

I didn't wait; I turned and ran.

"After him, lads! He's jumped ship!"

I ran three blocks with the sailors thundering right after me. I was able to dart between the people and the sedan chairs faster than they were, but I didn't know how much farther I could run. Then I turned down a narrow alley; a cart piled high with hay was moving slowly ahead of me with almost no room to get around. I started to squeeze past, and then had an idea. I jumped for the back and pulled myself up. Quickly, I dug under the hay and lay there panting.

"Where'd he go?" one of the sailors said as he came to a stop not an arm's length away from me. The wagon creaked slowly on over the cobblestone street.

"Did you see him?" said another.

"No. But he's got to be around here somewhere." It was Henson. "You there, check between those buildings. Then see if he went in that pub back at the corner. And you," he said to another sailor, "run ahead and see if you can see him."

Slowly, the cart was moving me to safety. Then it stopped. *Oh, no,* I thought. *Now they'll catch me for sure. Move on; move on! Oh driver, please move on.* But the cart stayed put.

"He's not in there, sir," said one of the sailors as they gathered around the back of the cart. Soon the others arrived to make their reports.

"Here, move out of the way, lads," said Henson. "The man wants to fork some hay into this shed. But check that shed first, Barclay."

I heard the driver pull a pitchfork off the front of

the cart. Then I heard it zing into the hay near me. My heart almost stopped. I was either going to be stabbed with the pitchfork or exposed to the crew of the *Dumfries*.

I was about to give myself up when Henson said, "When we catch that kid, we'll hang him from the yardarms. No one deserts a ship and lives to tell about it."

"What do you mean? We ain't her majesty's navy," another voice said. "Jumpin' ship's not a capital offense. Blokes do it all the time."

"Not when I'm first mate. Come on; let's go. We'll still get him."

Shunk. The pitchfork dug deep into the hay right near my head. Two of the prongs went on either side of my hand and lifted the hay away, and I could see the stars above. But still I stayed put.

Then I heard the sailors shuffle back down the alley, grumbling among themselves as they left. While they were looking the other way, and before the driver came back for another fork of hay, I crawled out and dropped over the side of the cart.

✧ ✧ ✧ ✧

Fearing the crew of the *Dumfries* more than the Imperial Chinese army, I decided to return to the Chinese city, keeping a sharp watch for any soldiers. But no one was specifically looking for me there as Henson had been in the European sector. In fact, no one had seemed to bother me in the Chinese city except when I strayed too near the fighting.

I slept that night on the cold steps of a Buddhist temple with the great idol rising high above me. In the morning I was stiff and sore, and so hungry I thought I must be close to starving. Some worshipers put bowls of rice and vegetables near the bottom of the Buddha. Another shuffling woman was with them. I began to wonder whether all Chinese women had little baby feet.

When the worshipers left, I went to investigate the food they had left. *Maybe, I could eat a little of it,* I thought. But there were always people nearby, and I realized it was an offering to their idol.

I tried begging, making foolish hand motions to try and communicate that I wanted something to eat. Many people refused to even notice me, but some laughed and encouraged me to do it some more. Maybe they thought I was putting on a show. But no one gave me food.

In the afternoon, I went down to the waterfront where I could see the *Dumfries* out in the harbor. A barge was alongside loading cargo aboard. The ship would be sailing soon. I considered turning myself in, maybe to the British consulate. Certainly, the authorities would protect me from being hung, and I didn't really think Captain Morris would allow that anyway. But I truly didn't want to spend an extra six to eight months at sea while the *Dumfries* sailed to San Francisco and back.

No, I decided, *I shall wait until she sails. Then I will go back into the European city and find a job on a ship sailing directly to England.* But, oh, I was so hungry.

And then, while I was staring out into the harbor, a young voice said, "You Englishman?" I turned to see a smiling Chinese girl just about my age. I noticed her smile because most of the Chinese did not seem to smile very much.

"Yes, I'm English." I was grateful to find someone—anyone—who wasn't threatening me or chasing me or making fun of me. "What's your name?"

"Me English."

"What?"

"You—me—English."

We fumbled around trying to talk to each other for a while until I figured out that she wanted me to teach her English. That gave me an idea. With a lot of difficulty, I got across that I'd teach her English if she would get me food.

The girl seemed delighted with that idea and hurried off, beckoning with her hand for me to follow her. The first thing I noticed was that she didn't have the tiny feet all the other Chinese women seemed to have. I pointed to her feet and made a sign with my hands that they were long. At first she blushed, but then she smiled and said, "English," nodding her head.

By pointing at ourselves and saying our names, I figured out her name was Namu and told her that mine was Neil. We didn't go far before we came to a large walled compound. *If this is her home*, I thought, *she comes from a very important family*. She took me around to a gate at the back and made me understand with hand motions, a flood of Chinese, and an occasional English word, that I was to wait there.

I waited and waited and was almost convinced that she had forgotten me or changed her mind when a unit of Imperial soldiers came marching down the street. I turned my back to them, hoping they wouldn't notice me, but just when they were even with me, the officer ordered them to stop. I heard his footsteps coming my way. He tapped me on the shoulder and said something in Chinese. I glanced from side to side to see if there was a chance to run, but I could see uniforms in both directions. Then, just when all seemed lost, the door in the wall squeaked open on its rusty hinges and Namu stood there smiling at me.

She bowed and said, "Neil," and beckoned for me to come in.

I turned and looked at the officer. To my amazement, he bowed to Namu and then rejoined his soldiers. It felt like a thousand pounds were lifted off me as they marched off.

Chapter 6

The Wreck of the Good Ship *Dumfries*

N AMU LED ME THROUGH A GARDEN to a small bamboo hut that had once been a stable. She motioned to me to sit down and then indicated with hand motions—and a stream of sing-song Chinese words—that she was going to her house for some food.

When she returned, I gobbled down the tasty rice, fish, and vegetables she had brought me. Gratefully, I began right in on her English lesson. Of course, for me, it was a Chinese lesson, too.

"Rice," I said, pointing to the last bite in my wooden bowl.

"Ra-SEE," she responded, nodding her head. But a moment later, when I had cleaned my bowl, I realized she had it wrong because she pointed to my empty bowl and said, "Ra-SEE," again.

That kind of confusion happened often that first afternoon, but we soon got better at communicating. I finally figured out that Namu's family name was Yang, but unlike the English, the Chinese put their family name first, making her full name Yang Namu. She was a very smart girl.

I was very grateful when she let me stay in the bamboo hut that night and showed me how to go in and out the door in the back wall.

The next morning I hurried down to the waterfront. The *Dumfries* still floated in the morning mist, and I could just make out workers transferring cargo onto the deck from a barge tied alongside. Disappointed, I realized it still wouldn't be safe for me to go into the European city.

I returned to the bamboo hut in Namu's garden and was surprised to find her crying. But she brightened up so quickly upon seeing me that I figured she thought I had left. All that day we worked on English until I was so bored I had to remind myself that I was working for my food. When I thought of it that way, it wasn't such a hard job.

The next morning, the *Dumfries* was gone, and I hurried to the British Consulate as fast as I could—keeping closer to the waterfront to avoid any Chinese soldiers. I decided that I would complain about having been shanghaied. Maybe they would send me back as a passenger and charge Aiken & Company for my passage for having shanghaied me in the first place.

I realized how dirty and bedraggled I was when

the clerk who let me into the beautiful government offices wrinkled his nose at me.

In a few minutes I was explaining my plight to a white-wigged official sitting behind a huge desk.

"We don't mediate crew complaints," he said without looking up from his paperwork.

"But I was shanghaied!" I protested.

"Not my concern."

"But how am I going to get home?"

"I have no idea." He looked up at me then, his eyebrows arched high but his eyelids nearly closed, giving him a very bored look. "Looks like you've got a problem," he said through his thin nose, "but it's not my problem, so run along and quit smelling up my office."

Trying for my alternative, I said, "Then can I sign on for a crew headed back to England?"

"Who knows?" he said, going back to his paperwork.

I asked him where I could apply, but he refused to answer me any further, so I finally left. On the way out, I asked the clerk where I could sign on for a ship's crew. He said I might try at the shipping company offices or catch some of the officers as they came ashore.

The idea of speaking directly to ships' officers scared me. *What if they shanghaied me again but weren't heading to England?* Then I realized that even someone in a shipping office might try to trick me into signing on the wrong ship if they were short-handed. So I decided that no matter who I spoke to, my first question would be, "Do you have a ship sailing directly to England in the next day or two?" If the answer was no, I wouldn't mention my interest in signing on as crew.

Down near the waterfront I found the row of shipping offices. There was Fleming and Company out of London, Turnbull out of Glasgow, Clyde & Australian Shipping Company, Brocklebank out of Liverpool, and many others. I stopped in each one without any luck, and then I came to Aiken & Company out of Liverpool—the owner of the *Dumfries*.

"Well," said the agent, scratching his whiskered chin and looking at a chart. "Next one's not due to sail for five weeks, but you should have been here yesterday. The *Dumfries* set sail for England on the morning tide."

"The *Dumfries?*" I gulped. "But I thought she was headed for San Francisco with a load of silk."

"Where'd you hear that?" The agent leaned forward and squinted his eyes at me. Then he relaxed and continued casually, "My, how news does fly. Unfortunately, rumors are not always up to date."

"What do you mean?"

The agent got up from his chair and walked to the office window. "It's true; we were having trouble getting tea at a profitable price, so we were going to send her to America with silk. But then, at the last minute, we made a good deal with some tea traders who got past the Red Turbans. So, she headed back to Liverpool this morning."

"W-what?" I stammered. I couldn't believe it. The *Dumfries* had gone back to England after all—and I had missed it.

"I *said*, 'She sailed for Liverpool this morning.'" Then he wheeled around like he was about to pounce on me. "How'd you know about the silk shipment?" he demanded. "Such details of the business are supposed to be secret."

Without thinking, I said, "Jeffries told me."

"Jeffries, the Negro steward? Hey . . . I know who you are," he glowered. "You're the *Dumfries'* cabin boy who jumped ship, aren't you?"

I nodded, speechless.

"Well, let me tell you something, young man." By now the agent was shouting. "Nobody jumps ship from an Aiken vessel. I'm gonna blackball you so you'll never work on another line out of Shanghai. Now get out of here!"

Outside the Aiken office, I sank to the cobblestone street, devastated. What had I done? I had jumped ship from the very vessel that could have taken me home sooner than any other. How foolish I'd been to be in such a hurry! But how could I have known? I had only acted on the information I'd been given. Maybe it was just my bad luck.

In fact, ever since I'd come to visit my grandparents in London, nothing had worked out right.

I had nowhere else to go, so that afternoon I stumbled back to the little bamboo hut in the Chinese city. Namu wasn't there and I was glad, because I finally couldn't hold back the tears. I think anybody would have cried if he found himself stranded all alone on the other side of the world.

✧ ✧ ✧ ✧

True to her word, Namu brought me food every day and I tried to teach her English. And every day for the next couple weeks I went down to the waterfront and made my rounds to the shipping offices. But the problem of the price of tea was real. The Chinese civil war had caused prices to rise, and for the time being almost all tea trade had stopped. The *Dumfries* had been the last clipper to sail with a profitable cargo.

The other ships were sitting in harbor waiting or had been diverted to Australia or America or even up to Japan in hopes of finding a cargo that would bring their owners more money.

"Maybe if we don't ship any tea to England for a while," said one of the agents, "tea will become so scarce there that its price will go up enough to cover our costs here and we can begin shipping again. But who knows when that'll be?"

Then one day the agent in the Clyde and Australian Shipping Company said, "Well, the *Geelong* is due in here any day now, and my guess is that she'll sail for London about May ninth."

"You think she needs any more crew? Is there a chance I could sign on?"

"Only Captain Bowers can answer that, but you look awfully young. You had any experience?"

"Sure. I was cabin boy on the *Dumfries*, but I learned a lot of other stuff while we were at sea."

"The *Dumfries*?" The man frowned. "Hey, you're the boy who jumped ship, aren't you. Forget it. We have no use for the likes of you."

That's how I learned what it meant to be blackballed. The Aiken agent had gone around to all the other companies and told them about me, so I couldn't get a job.

I began to feel panicky. Was I going to be stuck in China forever?

As I glumly walked back through the Chinese section of Shanghai, I recognized something familiar about the man in front of me. He wore the traditional Chinese clothes and had the common black pigtail hanging down his back, but his walk had a certain

bounce to it that reminded me of someone I knew. But who?

I hurried to catch up. As I got closer, the man turned and greeted someone, and I saw that he had lighter skin than most Chinese. And then I saw his eyes. They were gray-blue and seemed to be laughing.

I did know the man! It was Hudson Taylor, the young missionary who had sailed from England on the *Dumfries*, dressed for all the world like a Chinese man.

"Mr. Taylor, why are you dressed like that?" I blurted out.

Hudson Taylor

turned in surprise. "Well, if it isn't young Neil Thompson," he said with a wide grin on his face. "You like this?" he said, bowing as all the Chinese do when greeting people.

"But . . . but, how'd you get long black hair?"

Taylor put his finger to his lips and grinned again. "Shh. That wasn't hard. I dyed my own hair and am letting it grow. In the meantime, this is a fake pigtail." And he bent down to show me that it had been woven into his own hair.

"But why?"

The young man motioned for me to walk along with him. "I came here to tell the Chinese people about Jesus—not about English clothes and customs. I don't want the Chinese to reject the Gospel just because they associate Christianity with the white man's ways."

"But you won't fool any Chinese people once they get a good look at you," I snorted.

"I'm not trying to make anyone think that I *am* Chinese, but foreigners are hated in China these days, so why should I refuse to adopt Chinese ways as though my foreign ways were better? As long as one is modestly dressed, the kind of clothes one wears is not a moral issue."

"But I've seen some of the other missionaries, and they still wear European clothes."

"That's right. And do you know where they live?" he asked. Without giving me time to respond, he went on, "They live in the European sector and have very little daily contact with the Chinese."

"So where do you live?"

"Just down the street there, not far from the next bridge over the canal." Suddenly Taylor stopped and looked at me curiously. "But enough talk about me. Tell me how you come to be here, Neil. I feared you had drowned!"

"I didn't drown. I just jumped ship . . . and totally ruined my life," I said, looking down at the ground.

"What do you mean?"

Seeing Hudson Taylor had almost made me forget my troubles, but now they all came tumbling out. "I thought the *Dumfries* was sailing for San Francisco, and I didn't want to go because it would take a year and a half to get back to England, and I wanted to get home soon. But then the *Dumfries* sailed for England after all . . . and now no one will hire me because I jumped ship . . . and I don't have any money for passage." I sighed. "It was a big mistake."

"But you're alive!" cried Taylor. "And God can always redeem our worst mistakes."

"Of course I'm alive. Why shouldn't I be?" I asked glumly.

"I mean you didn't go down with the ship."

" 'Down with the ship'? What do you mean?"

"Didn't you hear?" he said. "The *Dumfries* sank!"

"It sank?" My head was spinning.

"Yes. It sank near the Pescadores Islands in the China Sea."

"It sank . . . . Were all hands lost?"

Taylor shook his head. "They don't know yet. Word came from another ship who spotted the wreck,

75

and there was no sign of life. But that's why I was so surprised to see you. . . . You're alive! You might think you made a big mistake, Neil Thompson, but I think God's been watching out for you."

I was dumbfounded. The *Dumfries* had gone down, and I would have been on it if I hadn't made a "mistake" and jumped ship. . . .

Chapter 7

Bound Feet and Sky Rockets

HUDSON TAYLOR INVITED ME to his house, and I gratefully followed. Even in his Chinese clothes and pigtail, Taylor was a link to home and I didn't want to lose it. But he lived not far from the north gate of the old city, and as the sun set I could again hear cannons and rifle fire as the fighting between the rebels and the Imperial army continued to our west.

Taylor's "house" was two rented rooms on the second floor of a plaster and stone bungalow with a stairway on the outside and a flat roof. "Those clothes of yours are getting pretty threadbare," Taylor noted as he lit a lamp. "How about my getting you something else to wear? You don't mind wearing Chinese clothes, do you?"

I didn't think I would mind, and it might even prevent the Imperial troops from stopping me on the street. Taylor told me that several Europeans were supporting the rebels—the Red Turbans, as they were called—so being seen walking around the streets of the Chinese city in European clothes made one a suspect. But when I tried on Taylor's Chinese clothes, the baggy pants and thin sandals felt very strange.

"You can stay with me while we try to figure out some way to get you back to England," Taylor offered.

Again I eagerly accepted. I appreciated how Namu had taken me in, and we were beginning to be able to communicate—a little English, a little Chinese—but I hadn't realized how much I missed the daily companionship of an English-speaking person.

That night the fighting was closer than ever, and I could hardly sleep. People were shouting and yelling, beating gongs, and blowing conch shells—besides the gunfire and rockets that kept up a fierce racket all night.

The next morning, after a bowl of cold rice, Hudson Taylor said, "Come with me. After all that fighting, I'm sure there's a lot for me to do." Then he grabbed a black bag and headed for the door.

"Have you decided to eat like the Chinese, too?" I grumbled as we went out the door.

"Why not?"

"Because I miss British cooking," I said. "After being on a ship for five months and then living on the streets for weeks, I was hoping for some familiar food."

"Hmm. I'll see what I can do."

Even at his young age—which I finally figured out was about twenty-two—Hudson Taylor had had some medical training (though he had not received his degree as a doctor), and his work for the morning was tending to the wounded civilians from the night's fighting. We didn't have to walk far to find them. I could hardly believe the destruction: whole houses had been blown away. Rubble and broken signs with colorful Chinese letters on them cluttered the streets. Crying children wandered around in the smoking ruins.

Taylor treated a woman who had a severe burn on the side of her head, then a man who had been shot through the shoulder. Next he found a little girl whose feet were badly injured. "Probably a rocket explosion," he murmured. "Would you get some clean bandages out of my bag, Neil?"

After working for a while trying to clean the small, bloody feet, he shook his head. "There's really very little left of her feet. The only consolation is that she probably won't have to endure the misery of having her feet bound for the rest of her life."

"Having her *what*?" I said.

"Having her feet bound." The little girl was whimpering pitifully as Taylor put some ointment on the raw wounds and bandaged them carefully. "With these terrible wounds, hopefully her parents won't bind her feet . . . if she still has any parents."

"Why would they bind up her feet?"

"It's the custom. They bind up little girls' feet so they won't grow. It's very painful for the child—cripples them, actually."

"But why?"

"I'm not sure. Some say the Chinese think small feet are beautiful. Some say it's the way Chinese men keep their women at home. You've probably seen the women shuffling around on tiny feet. They couldn't walk very far or fast if they wanted to . . . it's a terrible custom."

"Ha," I snorted. "I thought you were the one who defended Chinese customs."

Hudson Taylor closed his black bag and stood up. "Not all of them, Neil. There are many sad and wicked practices in this heathen land that I hope the Gospel of Jesus Christ will change. As for food and clothes—all I meant is that it's foolish to insist on white man's customs in China when Chinese customs serve just as well. But the Gospel judges us all—whether it's the cruel binding up of little girls' feet here in China or the white man's slavery of the black man. Fortunately, slavery has been outlawed in England, but it still continues in America. It's a very great sin, Neil. A very great sin."

✧ ✧ ✧ ✧

For the next three days I accompanied Hudson Taylor as he took care of the wounded. Then the fighting seemed to subside, and we were able to get some rest. I went to see Namu and told her I was living with a friend but that I would come and give her English lessons whenever I could.

That evening when I got to Hudson Taylor's place, the missionary put some boiled potatoes, cheese, and a small hunk of cold corned beef on my plate. I was delighted. "Mmm, where'd you get real food?" I asked, sinking my teeth into the corned beef. But Taylor didn't answer. He just sat at the table, not eating, looking gloomily at his plate.

"What's the matter?" I asked.

"What? Oh, nothing, really . . ." The young missionary picked up a fork and poked at his food. I bit into the cheese and waited. If Mr. Taylor wasn't hungry, I'd have been more than happy to help out with his share.

Finally he sighed. "I went into the European sector today—that's where I got the food." He took a bite of the potatoes and chewed thoughtfully. "I settled here in the Chinese city because that's where I feel I can do the most good," he said, almost as if trying to convince himself. "But it sure is lonely. At least in the European sector there are other people from home . . . familiar language, familiar ways."

I nodded. I knew what he meant about being lonely. I was enjoying the young missionary's company, but . . . England felt so far away, like a dream world that I'd only read about. I hadn't realized he felt like that, too. At least I was going to go back soon—I hoped—but Mr. Taylor had come to stay. Years, maybe.

"Maybe you ought to get married," I said, trying to be helpful. "A wife would be good company."

He choked on a potato—then he began to laugh. "Did you follow me today, you scamp?" He chuckled again. Then he leaned forward; his eyes brightened and he began talking excitedly. "In the European sector there is a school for girls run by a spinster missionary, a Miss Ann Aldersey. When I first arrived in Shanghai, I made it a point to go around and meet all the other missionaries here, and I met one of the young teachers there—her name is Maria, Miss Maria Dyer." He stopped and looked off into space, as if forgetting I was in the room.

"You like her?" I prompted.

"Well . . ." Hudson Taylor looked embarrassed. "I hardly know her, but she didn't seem put off by my Chinese dress. She's only nineteen years old, but she speaks excellent Chinese."

"How did she learn it?"

"Her parents were missionaries here, so she grew up in China. When they died, she joined Miss Aldersey's school for girls as a teacher. However, Miss Aldersey can't stand me. I've tried and tried to see Maria again—in fact, I tried again today! But Miss Aldersey runs that school with an iron hand. 'I won't have one of my respectable teachers seeing the likes of you,' she told me today. 'It would be the scandal of the Orient.'"

I laughed as he mimicked the spinster Miss Aldersey. "Still," I said, "you're not going to give up, are you?"

He grinned. "Probably not. Actually, Maria's legal guardian is her uncle in England. But Miss Aldersey rules the roost as far as she is concerned here in China."

I looked at Taylor's plate. Somehow in the midst of his thoughtful mood, he had managed to clean his plate. I had to give up my hopes for a second helping.

Hudson Taylor stood up abruptly and picked up the dirty plates, as if shoving his pleasant dream about Miss Maria Dyer off his lap. "But the main reason I'm in China is to bring the Gospel to the Chinese, not to go a-courtin'. Tomorrow, I'm going with one of the other missionaries who knows the Chinese language better than I do, and we're going to preach to the boat people on the Woosung River. You want to come?"

"Sure!" I said.

❖ ❖ ❖ ❖

The next morning we hired a small Chinese junk and its boatman and set out on the river. Seeing the ships in the harbor again made me ache for home. How was I ever going to get back to England?

We spent all day sailing around the harbor and up the river a short distance. We stopped wherever two or three junks were tied up, and Hudson Taylor and the other missionary tried to preach to the people. Most would stand on the decks of their boats and listen politely, but I could not tell if they had any real interest.

Having been at sea for several months, both Hudson Taylor and I had good tans on our faces and arms, but the other missionary was bright red with a severe sunburn by the time our day on the water was over. We sailed home in near darkness and were passing some of the large junks of the Imperial navy when gongs started sounding and the men on board began to yell at us.

Our boatman was terrified and yelled back in rapid Chinese. "They think we are rebel sympathizers and are threatening to sink us with cannon fire," the other missionary interpreted.

"Well, tell them we're not," Taylor ordered our boatman.

"He's been trying," said the missionary, "but they don't believe him."

Suddenly, Hudson Taylor began to sing a hymn at the top of his lungs. In the dim light, I could see the other missionary waving his hands to silence Taylor. Then the other man stopped, and after a moment, he joined in the singing, too. I realized they were trying to demonstrate with their English songs that they were indeed foreigners and not rebels. It was the first time I'd known Hudson Taylor to be glad to announce that he was a European and not Chinese. As soon as I understood what was going on, I tried to join in, too.

We must have sounded more like a bunch of cows bawling to be milked than a church choir, but no shots were fired, and we slowly slipped past. When it was clear that the Imperial navy wasn't going to

sink us, Hudson Taylor couldn't help himself and broke out laughing right in the middle of the chorus of the hymn. Pretty soon we were all laughing so hard we nearly tumbled out of our boat.

But that night the street fighting began again. This time it was very close. "Here," Taylor said as a rocket screamed overhead. "You better blow this up and keep it close by. We might need it."

It was a swimming belt, a strong balloon inside a canvas bag that was attached to a belt. "If they close the bridge or even blow it up, we may need to swim across the canal to the European sector," Taylor explained.

As the fighting approached, the rebels set up a cannon at the end of our street. That night the noise was terrible, and we awakened to a bright orange light shining through our window. Fire was raging through the wooden houses just a few doors away, whipped up by a strong breeze. We climbed up on the flat roof of the bungalow to get a better view. "We don't want to get cut off by that fire," said Taylor in a worried voice.

He pulled me down so that we were lying low on the roof because of the bullets splattering on the tile around us. Then in the middle of all the noise, I heard Hudson Taylor begin to pray aloud; as he prayed, the wind that had been whipping up the fire died down and a gentle rain began to fall.

Just then a cannon ball struck the roof of the house opposite us and sharp fragments flew all about us. "Let's get back inside," he said, "and try to get some sleep."

"*Sleep?*" I said incredulously.

"Well, God answered our prayer about the fire, so I think we can trust Him to take care of us for the rest of the night."

Somehow the bungalow was still standing the next morning. When dawn arrived, the fighting had subsided, and we risked a tour around our neighborhood. The streets were a total mess of rubble. Several contained nothing but smoldering ruins. But the big news was that the rebels had overrun our area of the city, driving back the Imperial forces. We were now in rebel-held territory.

Suddenly, the implications of our situation hit me: I could no longer freely travel to the European part of the city or to the waterfront where I could look for ships going back to England. There was one more barrier between me and home!

Chapter 8

The Tomb of the Living Dead

A S HE LOOKED AT THE DESTRUCTION all around us, Hudson Taylor murmured, "This is terrible, truly terrible. People always think their reasons for going to war are reasonable, but they seldom count the cost in terms of the dreadful suffering to the common people, like these poor folks here in the streets."

We helped a man put out a fire that was burning the last of his house. I don't know what good it did; there was nothing left for him to live in, but maybe he could rescue a few items from the ruins.

As we walked back to our apartment, Taylor said, "You know, Neil, God is always in control, and He can even use something evil like this for His good."

"I don't see anything good about it," I said, kicking some rubble out of my path. "It just makes my problem bigger: I can't get to the waterfront to look for a boat back to England."

"You shouldn't think of it that way, Neil. God will help you get home when the time is right. As for now, one good thing is that the interior of China is now open to the Gospel."

We climbed the stairs to the apartment and pushed open the flimsy door. "What do you mean?" I finally asked, as Taylor set a bowl in front of me for my breakfast. I grimaced—cold rice.

"The British treaty with the Imperial Chinese government says foreigners are not supposed to go inland into China," he explained, happily heaping rice into his own bowl. "And though many merchants do it anyway, we are supposed to stay in the coastal 'treaty' cities. But now we're in rebel-controlled territory; the Imperial Government is not in charge here. We can go wherever we want." He grinned. "I think I'll leave tomorrow. You want to come? I'll need someone to handle my luggage and medical supplies."

I slowly chewed the cold rice. There was no good reason to stay in Shanghai. No ships would hire me, and I couldn't even get to the waterfront. But the idea of going farther away from the port city worried me. What if something happened? What if I got sick? What if the front lines of the fighting suddenly changed and we were caught in Imperial territory and were put in prison?

When I asked Taylor about those risks, he

brushed them off. "One of the terms of the treaty between the Chinese and British governments is that if a British citizen is charged with anything, he or she has the right to be tried in a British court. So even if we were caught behind the lines, they'd have to bring us back here to Shanghai. Besides, we'll be back in a week or two."

The trip still didn't sound very safe to me, but the next morning I found myself trudging along the road behind Hudson Taylor with a large pack of his supplies on my back. He was carrying a load, too, but as the summer sun reached high noon, I was drenched with sweat and wondered why I ever agreed to this trip. The heat was nearly unbearable.

That afternoon we came to a canal and paid for passage on a junk. For two days we sailed on the canal that ran between checkerboard fields of rice stubble or brown earth ready for the next planting. From time to time we stopped at small villages where Hudson Taylor preached to the farmers and fishermen at the dock in his halting Chinese. This time we had no interpreter.

At the end of the second day, we left the canal and took a road heading up some nearby hills. Near the summit there was a pagoda; Taylor suggested we climb it. "Pagodas were originally built as watchtowers," he explained, "but now the Chinese people think they protect them from evil spirits."

From the top of the pagoda we were amazed to see the beautiful countryside that stretched out below us. There were fields of wheat, barley, peas, and

beans, all laid out like gardens. Streams, lined with graceful willow trees, could be seen meandering between the fields. Around the various farmhouses were fruit trees and graceful shade trees. In the hazy distance stood a majestic, walled city with the glint of gold-topped temples shining in the late afternoon sun.

"Inland China," murmured Hudson Taylor. "That is where God has called me. Look across that plain, Neil. China continues to the west for over two thousand miles, and there is no one to tell those millions of people about Jesus Christ."

I was worried that he might start hiking those two thousand miles right then, but then I remembered that he promised we'd be back in Shanghai in two weeks.

We stayed that night in a roadside inn halfway down the mountain and traveled on the next day to the walled city where Mr. Taylor intended to preach to the people. But each step of the way, I felt more and more anxious about getting farther from Shanghai. *What if, while I'm away, there's a ship that would take me back to England?* I worried. Fear of missing my ride became all I could think about. I *had* to find a way to get on one of those ships!

The winding streets of the city were narrow and crowded with people scurrying along underneath the overhanging balconies. Banners hung across the streets, and brightly painted signs announced the business of each shop. Over each door there was a mirror; it was so common that Mr. Taylor asked a merchant why everyone had one. "It is to scare off the evil spirits," he explained. "When the bad spirits see their ugly faces in the mirror, they will be frightened away."

When we came to a temple with its curved roof and snarling carved dragons on each corner, Hudson Taylor said, "This will be a good place to preach. People come here for religious purposes, so it will be good to talk to them here."

We put down our packs, and I helped him get out some tracts and booklets in Chinese to give to those who were interested. As I was unloading his pack and going through the valuable books and medicines he carried, an idea struck me: *These medical supplies are worth a lot of money . . . money that could be used to buy a ticket on a ship back to England.* And then my fingers touched a small leather pouch of coins. *More treasure here.*

I tried to push the idea out of my mind—Hudson Taylor was my friend, after all—but the thoughts would not leave me. How else was I going to get home? I had been blackballed with all the shipping companies for jumping ship; no one would hire me on as crew. Buying a ticket as a passenger was the only way! But I had no money, unless . . .

I began to scheme. First, I would have to find a time when I could take the supplies and the money without Hudson Taylor immediately knowing about it. Then, I'd have to find a place where I could sell the medicines. Almost anything foreign was valued by the Chinese people, but I would need to get top price, so I would need to find someone who knew the worth of the medical supplies. And finally, I'd need time to get far enough down the road back to Shanghai before Taylor suspected what had happened and could catch up with me.

It was all so unlikely that I allowed myself to dream about it, thinking of every detail, until finally it didn't seem so impossible—or bad.

Hudson Taylor was right about being able to attract listeners on the steps of the temple; as soon as he started to preach, several people gathered around him.

Usually, because of our Chinese dress, people did not take much notice of us in a crowd, but whenever we tried to speak, our difficulty with the Chinese language soon identified us as Europeans and people would look at us more closely. Since I had not seen any other white people in that city, I assumed the listeners were just curious.

However, once Hudson Taylor finished speaking, four Buddhist monks in their long yellow robes and shaved heads came out of the temple and began to ask about us. Mr. Taylor could have answered for himself, but he let one of his onlookers answer for him, repeating much of his message.

As well as I could understand, the man faithfully told how God loved them, that they were sinners, but that Jesus died instead of them and paid the penalty for their guilt.

"That's true, very true," said Taylor, obviously pleased that the man had been listening so carefully.

"Honorable teacher," said one of the monks, "please come into our temple and have tea."

They took us into the cool, dark interior of the temple where their living quarters were and had us sit down on thick satin cushions while we drank green tea. Flickering oil lamps provided the only light and the strong smell of incense drifted in the air. Mr. Taylor asked many questions about their monastery and whether they had ever heard of Christianity. They had; merchants had brought back reports from the coastal cities about the Christian religion that the white men preached, but they did not know who Jesus Christ was.

Finally, they asked, "Would you like to see our holy man? We are very fortunate to have him. He is showing us the way."

We were, of course, curious and followed the monks as they led us through a garden to a stone wall. "He is in there," one of the priests said as he pointed to a small hole in the wall not much larger than a man's hand.

First, Hudson Taylor and then I looked through the hole. What I saw, so dimly that at first I could not make it out, was the shadow of a man huddled in the corner. After a few more questions, we learned that there was no door or window in the cell. The man had been sealed into the tomb. The only light, air, water, or food he received was given to him through the hole in the wall.

"But why?" I said in my limited Chinese. "Why would he want to be in there?"

"To rid himself from sin," the monks said.

"Has he succeeded?" asked Taylor.

"For many years he has had no contact with other humans, so he cannot have sinned against anyone," the monks explained proudly.

"He may not have sinned against other people, but is not sin first of all an offense against God?" Taylor reasoned.

"Well, yes, that is true," admitted the monks.

"Then, even though he has not harmed any other human, maybe he has sinned in his heart toward God."

The monks nodded to one another. It was possible.

"There is a better way," continued Taylor. Then he told them that God understands that we are all weak and sin against one another and toward Him in our hearts. "So God decided to forgive us, but He is a perfect God who cannot stand sin."

All the monks agreed with that. Trying to become more holy was the goal of their religion. They agreed that it was the only way to enter paradise. So Hudson Taylor explained that Jesus Christ's death paid for our sin, so the debt was settled.

Hudson Taylor gave the monks tracts and portions of the Gospels, and before we left the temple with its great Buddha idol, the monks said they would think about what he had said. That pleased Hudson Taylor very much.

But as we walked down the steps, I couldn't help remembering the man in the tomb and his desire to escape sin. I knew that I had sinned lots of times. In fact, I had to admit that my idea of stealing Hudson Taylor's supplies and money was sin, but a lot of other people had done some pretty low-down things to me . . . like shanghaing me to China. I was desperate; I had to get home, whatever it took! But the question kept coming to me: *Was sin so terrible that a man would become the living dead to try to escape it?*

❖ ❖ ❖ ❖

We stayed that night in a small inn and set out again the next morning walking the streets of the city looking for good places for Hudson Taylor to preach to people—an open marketplace, a public garden, the steps of another temple.

We spent all day at it, and Taylor was becoming exhausted when we were met by an unusual procession. First came two men with gongs, then came men with huge red caps and carrying flags. Following them walked a man with a large shade umbrella in front of the largest, fanciest sedan chair I had ever seen, carried by four men.

When they set the chair down—it was a fully enclosed chair with little curtains over the windows—out stepped a mandarin (a local official of the Imperial Chinese government). The rather stout gentleman wore long satin robes embroidered with the finest gold threads and studded with sparkling jewels.

He bowed respectfully and asked whether our journey had been pleasant. Then he looked at some of Hudson Taylor's books and pronounced them to be very fine books. He gave us several other compliments and made more polite conversation, then he said, "I am very glad to make your acquaintance, but the honorable travelers must go no farther."

"Thank you," said Taylor, "but we have business ahead."

"I would not want any unpleasantness to come to you," said the mandarin, "but if you were to travel on, you might discover how truly unpleasant the Imperial soldiers can be."

"I do not worry," said Hudson Taylor. "The Imperial forces have been driven back by the rebels."

"I know nothing of that," said the mandarin, "but here the local militia has not been overthrown, and it would be to your sorrow to discover what they are like."

"Thank you for your kind counsel, but we must be going." And with that, Hudson Taylor lifted his bag and moved on down the street.

Not knowing what else to do, I followed along, but when we rounded the next corner, several soldiers were standing about in the street. Upon seeing us, they surrounded Hudson Taylor and grabbed him roughly. "Foreign dog!" they yelled, and began to drag him off.

Taylor dropped his bag and called, "Neil, go back to the inn! Take all our luggage there and wait for me until I'm free." And then he was gone.

It all happened so fast that I didn't know what to think. Was the mandarin right? Was Hudson Taylor in real trouble? Or were they just harassing him?

Then I remembered what Taylor had said about the rights of British citizens in China. Maybe he would be all right. I stooped to pick up his dropped bag. But both packs were too heavy for me to carry at one time; should I just leave one on the street and come back for it? And then I noticed that the shop nearest me looked something like a pawn shop, a place that might buy and sell all kinds of things.

Suddenly I realized I had my opportunity: I was alone with the supplies. As far as I knew, Hudson Taylor might get thrown into prison for a couple of weeks—or even months. I could not be expected to wait. *In fact,* I reasoned to myself, *I might do him the most good by hurrying back to Shanghai to report his arrest. He needs help.* And here was just the kind of shop that might buy the books and medical supplies. The possibility of having enough money to buy passage on a ship to England seemed within my reach.

Chapter 9

Betrayal in the Walled City

E VEN THOUGH HUDSON TAYLOR'S BOOKS were in English, the shop owner was glad to buy them as a curiosity, and he was willing to pay for the luggage, extra clothes, and some of the other items, too. But he said he had no use for Taylor's Chinese tracts and Scripture portions. When it came to the medical supplies, he offered me far less than I thought they were worth.

"I need a fair price for them," I said to the tall man. He looked even younger than Hudson Taylor.

"But I can't use them," he answered. "I would have to find some druggist or doctor to buy them. Who knows how much they would pay."

"Where can I find a druggist?" I asked.

The man shrugged. "Maybe down the street," and

he drew for me the Chinese character that would identify the druggist's sign.

It was nearly dark when I set off to find a better buyer. I was worried that the same soldiers who had arrested Hudson Taylor might be on the lookout for me, so I stayed in the shadows as much as possible.

When I came to the shop with the druggist sign, everything was dark. Most Chinese shop owners live above or behind their small stores, but no matter how hard I knocked, I could not raise anyone. I asked a passerby where another druggist was. Apparently, the only other druggist shop was some distance across the city, but what else could I do? *Maybe I shouldn't be selling Taylor's things*, I thought. *But I've already started, so I can't quit now.*

I tried to follow the complicated directions as well as I could but soon got hopelessly lost. I kept asking for directions and was sent down first one street and then another, until I came around a corner as I had been directed, and there was the sign . . . but it was the sign for the first shop I had gone to, the one where no one was home.

In despair, I went back to the pawn shop, resigned to accept the price the man had offered me the first time. The shop was dark, but after knocking on the door for some time, the man finally came to answer it with a small lamp in his big hand.

"I'm so sorry," he said when I told him what had happened. "I have been thinking about your medicines, and I'm not sure that I have any use for them. I am no doctor. How do I know that they are any good? A doctor or druggist might know, but I don't. What if I can't sell them? They are no good to me."

"But they are good, and I've got to sell them. I need the money," I protested. "You said you'd buy them."

"That was then. This is now. I've reconsidered," he shrugged.

I turned and began to walk away.

"But I'll tell you what I will do," he called after me. "I can see you are a good boy, so I'll do my best for you. I'll give you half price—half of what I offered you before."

"Half price? But that's robbery. Your earlier offer was too low."

"I wish I could do more," he said with an evil glint in his eye, "but even at that I'm taking a risk."

I quickly tried to calculate how much money I would have. With what he had paid me earlier and Taylor's little pouch of coins, half price for the medical supplies would bring me to about forty British

pounds or $200 if I sailed on an American ship. It would be tight, but I figured that ought to be enough, so I agreed. What else could I do?

The shopkeeper smiled and paid me. Then he bowed deeply, almost too deeply, I thought, as if he were mocking me.

I headed for the door.

At last I was on my way to England.

❖ ❖ ❖ ❖

It took more than an hour to get across the city to the gate in the east wall. There two rough-looking guards stopped me. "We close the gates at dark," one said. "Why would anyone want to travel at night. Are you running away from something?"

"No, not at all," I lied.

"Then where are you going?"

"To Shanghai."

"Shanghai? You're a fool. There are robbers on the road. Go home and wait until morning."

"But I must leave now. Just open the gate."

"What? It's a lot of work to open those heavy gates. We're paid to open them once in the morning and close them again at night. Who's going to pay for us to do all that extra work to open them now?"

I could see that they were after a bribe, but I was so short on money that I didn't want to pay one. "Isn't there some little door in the wall where you can let me out? You wouldn't have to open the whole gate."

"Well, yes, but we can't leave our post to show it to you," said the shorter of the two.

"Here," I said, finally holding out a couple coins.

"Oh, that's hardly worth it. What if the captain were to come around? We'd be in big trouble."

I added two more coins, and they smiled and grabbed them. "All right, the door's right there," they said, pointing to a dark alcove not more than six feet away. "You can open it for yourself." They roared with a big belly laugh as I went through and shut it behind me.

It made me angry to have been such a sucker, but what else could I have done? At least I was out of the city, and with such a beautiful, warm night, I couldn't stay angry for long.

I trudged down the road feeling very cocky. Without a pack, I figured I could travel all night and be over the hills and down to the canal by noon the next day. There I would again have to part with some of my precious money, but traveling by junk would be the fastest way to Shanghai. If I tried walking the whole distance, it would take longer and I'd have to spend money on food and places to sleep for several nights. Might as well sleep on a junk and get there faster.

The moon rose and the peaceful garden of the day before turned into a mysterious silver landscape. Here and there in the distance, I could see the dim orange glint of a lamp in a farmhouse window. But instead of giving me a feeling of the comforts of home, the lamps reminded me how far away from home I was. I was a stranger in a strange land, and I had left my only friend back in the walled city, possibly in prison.

But going for help is the best way to help him, I told myself.

But really, my conscience argued back, *you're just doing it for yourself, and you've stolen all his belongings in the process. How will he get home?* It didn't make me feel very good about myself, but there was no time to turn back . . . or was there?

Suddenly, I became aware of a shadow following me at some distance. *Maybe it's Taylor,* I thought. *Maybe he's been released and found out I left the city.* The idea sent shivers of fear through me. He would know I'd been a coward, thinking only of myself. On the other hand, the thought of his catching up with me was strangely comforting. I could get it all out in the open and be done with the sorry mess.

But I wasn't sure it was Taylor. It was most likely some other traveler just happening to be going in the same direction. *I wonder if the gate guards forced him to pay a bribe?* I thought.

I picked up my pace, not really wanting a stranger to travel with me—there would be too many questions.

But the shadow followed just as fast.

I began to run.

The shadow ran, too.

I ran faster, and the shadow began to gain on me.

We were going through open country with nothing but rice paddies on both sides of the road. There was nowhere to hide.

Finally, the follower caught up with me and ordered me to stop. It was not Hudson Taylor's voice!

I was so exhausted from running that I couldn't have taken another step, so I stopped and turned toward my follower.

The man was puffing as hard as I was, but he carried a big stick. We stood there facing each other, panting. Finally, he said, "You can give me that money now, boy." I realized then that he was the shopkeeper to whom I had sold Hudson Taylor's things.

"Why?" I asked.

"Just give it to me and be on your way."

There was no way I was going to give him that money. I turned and took off at top speed. He came thundering after me. I thought I was a good runner, but I was no match for someone older and bigger than me. I couldn't fool him by zigzagging; he kept a steady pace going right down the center of the road just a few yards back. And I could hear that he was slowly gaining on me again.

His breath was coming in great gasps, but so was mine. I could hear his feet sometimes stumble on a rock or in a rut and he would curse, but I also stumbled and almost went down.

I kept looking for something off to the side, maybe some ditch to hide in—anything to gain an advantage. And then I saw it: the silver reflection of the moon in a canal. I could swim. Maybe he couldn't swim, and I could lose him that way.

I dodged off the road hoping I wouldn't step in some hole in the dark. He was almost on me. I was thirty yards from the canal, then twenty. He was almost keeping up stride for stride.

And then, wham! I went down. He had reached out and stuck his stick between my legs and tripped me.

What little wind I had was completely knocked out of me, and I nearly blacked out. I looked out to the side to see him circling me with his big stick raised.

"The money," he gasped, "or I'll use this on you!"

By then, I believed he meant it.

I pulled out my fat little pouch and handed it over. In a moment he was gone, disappeared into the night.

I just lay where I had fallen and cried and slept and cried until morning. The whole trip had become a disaster, and I had no one to blame but myself. I was a robber and had been robbed. I had betrayed and was, in turn, betrayed. Now I was in no better shape than I had left Hudson Taylor in.

Chapter 10

The Long Road Back

WHEN THE SUN FINALLY CAME UP over the hills, I roused myself and staggered to the canal to wash my face. I had no idea what I was going to do now, or how I was going to get back to Shanghai, or how I was going to get on a ship headed to England. But as I thought about it, I realized that I should have done what Hudson Taylor had told me to do in the first place: I should have gone back to our inn and waited until he was released.

But it was too late now. I had ruined everything. There was no going back. And I couldn't just stand there in the middle of nowhere. Finally, I headed down the road toward Shanghai. Without money and hope, however, the way seemed twice as hard, and I had to force myself to put one foot before the other to travel over the mountain. I hardly noticed the great Pagoda at the summit.

When I got to the other side, I had no money to ride on a junk, so I began walking along the levee beside the canal. At night, I found a dark corner or bush to hide in and fell asleep, exhausted. I walked day after day, asking people along the way whether I was still on the road to Shanghai. My feet were blistered and sore and I was nearly starved. The only food I was able to eat were some peaches I stole off a farmer's tree and a dead, partially rotten fish I found along the canal bank.

One morning I woke up under the tree where I had fallen asleep and realized that I was very sick. Maybe it was the rotten fish, maybe it was the bad water I'd been drinking, maybe it was malaria. I didn't know, but I had a terrible fever. I staggered to my feet, however, determined to go on because there was no help for me there.

I have no idea how long I walked in the hot sun, but when I stopped a farmer driving an ox cart and asked how much farther it was to Shanghai, he said, "A very long way, if you keep walking in that direction. The road to Shanghai is behind you."

I could not tell whether I had passed the turn-off or whether—having awakened with a fever—I had started out walking in the wrong direction.

He saw how puzzled I looked and that I didn't feel well. "Would the honorable young man like a ride? I could take you as far as the turn-off."

I bowed and gratefully got on the back of the cart.

After a couple of hours he stopped and pointed down a road going in a new direction. I thanked him and turned to go. He called after me. "Here, I think you could use this more than I can," and he gave me his large, round bamboo hat.

The hat was a lifesaver that day as I staggered along under the hot sun.

Late in the afternoon, I began walking past more and more houses, until I realized that I was coming into the outskirts of Shanghai. I tried to pick up my step, eagerly looking forward to getting something to eat and sleeping in my bed at Taylor's apartment that night.

I decided that I would get my things and move out the next day. I didn't want to be there when he got home because he would surely have me arrested for the robbery.

A bright pink glow was still in the western sky when I turned down Taylor's street that evening. The fever made my body ache and everything seemed very eerie. I walked along almost in a daze, and then suddenly I was there . . . or I thought I was. But I wasn't there. It was not Taylor's house. In fact, there was no house at all—just a pile of stones and rubble.

I looked around. Maybe in my confusion I had taken the wrong turn. But no, the north gate of the old city and the bridge over the canal leading to the European sector was nearby. I had to be in the right place. It was just that Hudson Taylor's house had been blown up.

Down the street I saw a squad of Imperial troops

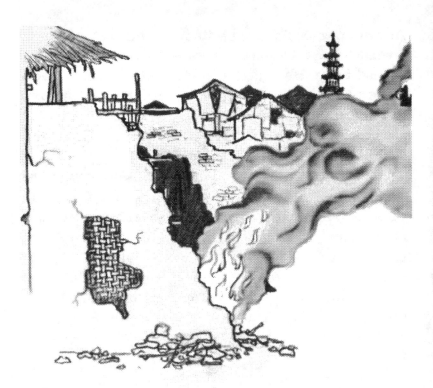

dragging three prisoners along by their pigtails. "No, no, no," cried one. "Don't let them kill me."

"What's happening?" I managed to ask a small boy who went running by toward all the action.

"They're going to chop their heads off."

"But why?" I called after him.

"They're rebels!"

So. The Imperial forces had retaken the city. As I looked around, I could see that the destruction had been tremendous. It wasn't just Mr. Taylor's apartment that had been blown away. Most buildings were in ruins, and those walls that were still standing had holes in them or were burned. Only here and there was a house or shop that had survived.

Exhausted, I sat down and must have fallen asleep because it was completely dark when some-one—or something—turned me over. A mangy dog was pulling at my shoulder and growling softly. Suddenly, the thought occurred to me that he was going to eat me. I had heard that the wild street dogs sometimes chewed on the bodies of people killed in the fighting before they were taken away for burial the next morning.

I jumped up and yelled at the thing. It ran off yelping, its tail between its skinny legs.

The next morning I made my way through once familiar streets that now looked strange by the wreckage of war. Hundreds of homeless people milled about. Some were wounded. Some appeared unhurt but were walking around aimlessly with a blank stare in their eyes.

It crossed my mind that I probably looked much the same even though the cause of my ruin was my own doing and not the war.

I had no idea what to do next, but finally decided to go to Namu's house, hoping that it would still be standing and that she would take me in again. But when I got there, my hopes were smashed. The gate in the back wall was standing open and many people were inside the compound. I peeked through the gate and saw that a kind of hospital had been set up in Namu's garden. All around the edge, awnings had been rigged from the garden wall to provide shade for the wounded.

And then, with a great relief, I saw Namu. She was one of the people attending to the wounded. I walked slowly over to where she was helping an old woman drink some water from a tin cup. "Namu?" I ventured.

She turned and ran to me. "Neil! I thought you dead. Mr. Taylor's house . . ." She clapped her hands. ". . . no more. I thought you dead."

I told her that we had gone on a long trip and that I was a little sick but okay.

"You eat?" she asked.

It was only plain rice—not even any vegetables—but for once I was very grateful for the white, sticky food.

For the next few days, I stayed with Namu, helping to care for the wounded and homeless and getting a little food and a place to sleep in return. I slept in the corner of the garden wall under one of the makeshift awnings like everyone else. There were several people who cared for the wounded. Some stayed there and some came and went each day—probably staying at their own homes—but no one bothered to ask me who I was or why I was there.

❖ ❖ ❖ ❖

After two weeks, the garden was nearly cleared out. Many of the wounded had died. Some had recovered and left, and others who were more severely wounded had been transferred to better places for

their care.

I was feeling better, too. My fever was gone and my strength had returned, but my spirits were lower than ever. After Hudson Taylor's apartment had been destroyed, I didn't even have any European clothes to wear to go to the waterfront and try to get a job on a boat. I was proud to be able to speak Chinese pretty well by this time, but I probably looked and acted like a Chinese person too. It was not very likely that a ship's captain would hire me.

Then one day Namu brought me a letter. "This letter came addressed to me, but inside it is in English. Can you read it to me?"

I opened the letter with curiosity and immediately noticed that it was signed by Hudson Taylor, and written to me.

Master Neil Thompson:

If this letter finds you, then I have guessed correctly as to your whereabouts.

I am happy to report to you that after being detained by the mandarin for only one day, I was released with no punishment. However, as you can imagine, I was not happy to discover by asking around that you had sold all my things the night before and left town.

I cannot imagine why you would abandon me, let alone steal from me. Did you not realize that I had no means of returning to Shanghai? I did not have enough money for fare on a junk or for food and lodging if I took the slower way home of walking. Fortunately, God took care of me and arranged for a speedy mail boat to carry me to Shanghai faster than I could have

*traveled by any other means. And the boatmen did not
even charge me.*

*I could have you arrested, and have often felt
tempted to do just that. However, Christ commands us
to return good for evil, so I will not harm one hair of
your head. I do not understand why you did what you
did, but I do forgive you.*

*My house was destroyed by the fighting the night
before I arrived, . . .*

I suddenly realized that by traveling in a fast
mail boat, Hudson Taylor had arrived in Shanghai
several days before I had. Maybe God *was* taking
care of him. I read on.

*. . . and since there are so few houses remaining in the
Chinese city, I am living at present in the English
sector. I have a small apartment, but there is still room
for you if you would like to return and stay with me.*

*I forgive you, Neil. Please accept my forgiveness. I
would like to see you again.*

Sincerely yours,
J. Hudson Taylor

I couldn't believe my eyes.

At first I thought it must be a trick. Taylor was
going to have the law on me once I turned up, I
figured. But then I realized that if he knew where I

was, he could have had me arrested at Namu's house at any time. Maybe it wasn't a trick after all.

I folded the letter and put it in my pocket.

"Read letter?" said Namu.

I tried to explain that the letter was actually for me. She could not understand that until I said it was from Dr. Taylor. Then she realized it must indeed be for me.

My hopes began to rise. Finally, I had a place to live again. Hudson Taylor said I could come and live with him. But that day passed and the next, and I still didn't go to see him or even answer his letter.

I intended to, but I just couldn't.

That evening, the flies and the dust in Namu's trampled garden were particularly unpleasant. *Why don't I go? What's the matter with me?* I wondered. It made no sense to stay there. I was miserable, and I wasn't really needed anymore. I set my mind to figuring out why I hesitated, and finally the word "guilty" came to me. I felt too guilty to face Hudson Taylor.

I thought of the holy man in the tomb and understood how someone could want to disappear when he or she had done a great wrong. But even though that's exactly what I felt like doing, I knew that crawling into a hole would do no good.

I kept the letter from Taylor and read it day after day. *Hudson Taylor says he forgives me, so why don't I feel forgiven?* I wondered. Maybe it was because what I had done was such a low-down thing. It was too awful to be forgiven.

Chapter 11

Tornado Lovers

ONE DAY NAMU SUGGESTED that I could make money by calling for sedan chairs. "Not much money, but Europeans pay . . . pay tip—I think you call it—just for getting them a ride."

"What do you mean?" I asked.

"Someone need sedan chair ride, and you go get sedan chair. They pay you."

"They would pay me?"

"Yes, yes. I've seen them do it. Come; I'll show you."

She grabbed my hand and started running down the dusty street toward the bridge into the European sector. I was nearly out of breath when she rounded a corner and nearly skidded to a stop. "There," she said pointing to a small Chinese boy standing by the door of one of the government buildings. "He's a runner."

He looked more like a beggar to me, and I said so to Namu.

"Look at Neil," she said, laughing.

I looked down at my clothes, the same ones I'd been wearing for weeks. They were stained and ragged. "I guess you're right," I said. "I suppose I look like a beggar, too."

Still, I hesitated. "What if someone recognizes me?" I was thinking about having robbed Hudson Taylor. True, his letter had said he would forgive me, but what if he had changed his mind? Or what if he told someone else about the robbery and that person decided to have me arrested? Daily contact with the English seemed risky.

But Namu assured me that Europeans were not that observant. "Chinese know you are not Chinese, but the English? They look at us without really seeing us. It is not honorable, but it is good for you. No one will notice."

Right then as we talked, a large, overweight Englishman came out of the building and the boy ran down the street to hail a sedan chair for him. And just like Namu had said, when he brought one back, the man gave the boy a small coin before getting into the chair.

That day I gave it a try, although it was hard to find people who needed rides that did not already have boys waiting to fetch chairs for them. Still, I had one advantage: I knew English—though I tried

to talk
in the bro-
ken way Namu
spoke to sound like
I was Chinese.

Once the Europeans knew that I understood English, they would often say, "I'll need a chair in an hour," or "Have three chairs here tomorrow morning." I got a lot of work that way.

At first this business gave me the hope that I could save enough money to buy my passage back to England on a ship. But when I realized that even the best days brought me no more than a small handful of pennies, my heart sank into despair again. It would take a year or two to save enough for a ticket, and in the meantime I had to spend some of my money on food.

However, hailing sedan chairs helped me learn my way around the European part of Shanghai and I soon began to recognize many of the people in the city. I even found the location of Miss Aldersey's girls' school, and soon figured out who Miss Maria Dyer was, the young teacher Hudson Taylor was sweet on.

As I became familiar with the homes and offices of the missionaries, I discovered where Hudson Taylor was living in the home of some missionaries named Jones. I figured out where Taylor lived as much to be able to stay away from him as anything. Namu was right; the English did not really pay attention to the Chinese people. They just looked past me or through me as though I weren't really there. As Namu said, it was not an honorable habit. In fact, it made me feel like a nobody, certainly a very disrespectful way of relating to someone.

But I knew Hudson Taylor was different—and that made me afraid. He cared about the Chinese as individual people, not just the "yellow masses." If he got close enough to look me in the face, he would certainly recognize me. So I stayed away from the new place where he lived . . . though sometimes I stood and gazed at it from a distance, wondering if he really would forgive me—and missing his friendship.

Then one day a set of strange circumstances hatched a new plan in my head. I called a sedan chair for a missionary woman. Even though it was morning, she was dressed up in fancy clothes as if she were going to an evening concert. Just before she got in, she said to me, "I'm going to Reverend and

Mrs. Joneses' house for tea and our ladies' prayer meeting. I will want a sedan chair when it is over. Have one waiting for me about two o'clock."

"Yes, ma'am. Will many ladies be attending?"

"I expect nearly everyone," she said absently as she got in and was carried off.

I followed along, making plans for how I might call several sedan chairs later in the day. When I got to the Joneses', I hung back, not wanting to be seen by Hudson Taylor if he was there. In a few minutes I noticed the stern Miss Aldersey and her young teachers from the girls' school arriving on foot. Miss Maria Dyer—Hudson Taylor's "sweetheart," as I thought of her—was among them.

I was not far from the Joneses' gate when Mrs. Jones came out of the house to greet the ladies. In the exchange of greetings, Miss Aldersey asked, "Is your dear husband at home today?"

"No," said Mrs. Jones. "He and Hudson Taylor are preaching this morning over at the Jesus Hall. But they should be back home sometime this afternoon."

At the mention of Hudson Taylor's name, Miss Aldersey stiffened and walked on past Mrs. Jones with her nose in the air. Hudson Taylor had certainly been right about her dislike of him.

As I waited around, another idea popped into my mind: Hudson Taylor couldn't possibly be angry with me anymore if I were able to arrange a meeting between him and the woman he loved. My thoughts raced. If I could only get them together, then maybe I could earn back Taylor's favor.

I sat down under a tree at the side of the street and tried to think of a plan. *Maybe I could have a sedan chair pick up Miss Dyer and take her to the place where Hudson Taylor is preaching*, I thought. But there would be no good reason for her to get into a chair if she did not call for one, and the women from the girls' school had walked. *What if I wrote her a note asking her to meet him somewhere and signed Hudson Taylor's name?* I got out Taylor's letter to me and tried to imagine if I could copy his writing style . . . not very likely. Besides, that would be dishonest, and if I wanted to get back on the good side of Hudson Taylor, I knew that I had to clean up my act.

I thought and thought, but still couldn't come up with a good plan.

From inside the Joneses' house I could hear the women singing hymns as someone played on the piano. They sounded like a choir of angels, and for a moment I remembered sitting beside my mother in church back in England as the beautiful music washed over us. I had a sudden longing to attend church again . . . but I shook the feeling away. That seemed so unlikely now.

As the morning wore on, huge clouds boiled up and the sky became terribly dark. A severe storm was approaching from the southeast across the river. I could just see the harbor from the street, and on one of the newly anchored ships, the sailors were up in the rigging. From this distance, the men looked like ants crawling around on the yardarms as they worked furiously to furl sails that had been left free to dry. It was going to be a bad storm.

The wind became hot and moist as the storm approached. Everything was quiet and sticky, and then from the bottom of the dark clouds across the river I saw an angry wisp of gray cloud snake down toward the ground. It nosed around like the trunk of an elephant trying to pick up a peanut, and whenever the twister touched the ground, its whole length turned black.

My eyes widened. *A tornado!*

The monster danced along, sucking up dark earth and debris, then slid down the hill toward the river. I was fascinated and terrified at the same time. The river was very wide at this point, but what if it came across the river and tore into the city of Shanghai? I started looking for nearby places where I could run for cover. The only thing I could see was a little stone bridge over a duck pond in a park just down the street. I started toward the bridge, keeping my eye on the twister as it marched across the river.

Over the water, it became a silver waterspout, sucking up the river like it had sucked up dirt on the land. The eerie funnel was still probably a mile away from me, but I could already hear its angry roar—a haunting, shrieking sound that grew steadily louder.

I began running for the stone bridge when I saw the spout head straight for a Chinese junk—a rather large ship, actually. One minute the junk was there, and the next it was gone. I didn't actually see it get sucked up into the twister. It was just there, and then it was gone. But in the split second that the funnel had approached the junk, I got some idea of the size of the thing. It was monstrous! I think it could have easily picked up a British battleship.

I dove under the bridge just as the wind picked up a furious force. I huddled there in the mud with a couple frightened ducks as the thought went through my mind: *What would you do if a tornado came at you while on board a ship at sea?*

❖ ❖ ❖ ❖

Witnesses later said that the twister missed the city and turned and skipped right up the center of the river, sucking up tens of thousands of gallons of water as it went. I believed them because a few minutes after I had taken cover under the bridge, it began to rain like I've never seen in all my life. It was dirty rain, full of mud and grass and sticks. Later I saw dead fish in the streets, probably drawn up with the river water and then dropped from the sky.

It rained so hard that within fifteen minutes the duck pond flooded the muddy area under the little bridge where I had taken refuge. I was scared to come out, but there was no alternative; I would drown if I stayed.

Even though my bamboo hat—which I had tied securely under my chin—diverted some of the rain, the water was coming down so hard that I felt like I was gasping for air.

Then, as fast as it had begun, the storm passed. Behind the clouds, the sky opened to brilliant sunshine, and it seemed like a whole new world.

In some ways, that was not an exaggeration. So much rain had fallen that the street had become a river of water nearly up to my knees. I sloshed along amazed at how different things looked.

When I got to the Joneses' house, the women were all out on the porch, chattering excitedly and pointing to the flood all around them. Even though it wasn't yet two o'clock, I offered to hail sedan chairs for them. There was obviously no way any of those ladies in their pretty dresses could wade home on their own.

They quickly accepted my offer, and I started calling for chair after chair.

It was then that a plan for getting Hudson Taylor and Miss Maria Dyer together clicked in my mind. Mrs. Jones had said that her husband and Taylor would be coming home before too long. With such a terrible storm, it seemed likely they'd be rushing home any time now. So, pretending to be honoring the "older" women first, I made sure that Miss Aldersey got a chair while young Miss Maria remained behind on the porch for a later ride.

But when all the other women had been whisked away, I waved off any more chairs, telling the coolie carriers that they were needed elsewhere in the city.

Poor Maria Dyer was left behind, standing on the porch with Mrs. Jones.

I took up a watch a short distance away. Sure enough, Reverend Jones and Mr. Taylor soon came sloshing back to the house. Even from a distance I could see Hudson Taylor's face light up. I knew it was just the opportunity he'd been waiting for. I saw the Joneses invite the two young people into their home to talk. I waited around outside for what seemed like hours. Things couldn't have been going too badly because Maria did not leave, but I was curious. What was happening in there?

It was nearly dark when Hudson Taylor, Maria, and the Joneses came out on the porch. They were talking and laughing so freely that I knew things had gone well. But I had no idea how well until Reverend Jones asked, "What date have you set for the wedding?"

Wedding?

"We will not set a date until I receive permission from my uncle in England," said Maria shyly.

"But after that," said Taylor, "you will be the first to know, my friend." Then he grabbed Maria around the waist and kissed her . . . right there on the porch.

I became foolishly bold then and stepped out from behind the bush that had concealed me. "May I call you chair?" I called in my pretended broken English.

"You can call me a chair or a table or anything you please," roared Hudson Taylor, unable to hold back his laughter. "But tonight I am most definitely a man, and the happiest man in China, at that."

Then he leaned forward, peering through the evening shadows, and yelled sharply, "Is that you, Neil Thompson?"

I gulped. "Yes, sir. It is."

"Well, come over here and meet my fiancée, Miss Maria Dyer."

I opened the gate and splashed slowly up the muddy path. I went through the motions of greeting her but was so scared at having been found out that I hardly knew what I was saying. Then I heard Taylor saying, "Run along and get Miss Dyer a sedan chair."

As I ran down the path, I heard him call after me,

"By the way, were you the one who called all the chairs for the ladies earlier?"

"Yes, sir."

"It figures," he said. "Listen, I want you to come back here and talk to me when you're done."

Oh, no, I thought. *Now I'm really going to get it.*

Chapter 12

Passage on the *Geelong*

ONCE MARIA WAS SITUATED in a sedan chair and on her way back to Miss Aldersey's school for girls, Hudson Taylor turned to me. "Maria says you didn't seem to want to call a chair for her earlier when all the other ladies left. Is that so?"

"I guess so," I said.

"I see," he said, rubbing his chin and looking very thoughtful.

The Joneses then said good night and went inside, leaving us standing alone on the street. Hudson Taylor turned again to me and said, "Do you feel better now?"

"B-better about what?" I stammered, staring at my mud-splattered feet and leggings. After a few moments of trying to play dumb, I said in a small voice, "You mean about running away with your things?"

"That's right. Do you feel better now that you've done something wonderful for me?"

I thought about it. I was happy about getting Mr. Taylor and Miss Dyer together at last . . . but, no, I didn't feel any better. I still felt awful about what I had done. "No," I admitted. "It was a terrible thing that I did."

"Yes, it was. But didn't you get my letter? I have forgiven you."

I shrugged, not knowing what to say. I had thought about it so many times. My hand absently pulled out the letter Hudson Taylor had written to me, but I still didn't feel forgiven. The guilt still hung over me like a great weight, and, to tell the truth, I didn't feel very comfortable talking to him right then.

Finally he said, "Neil, there's a reason why you don't feel any better. No matter how long you try to hide from me or how much you try to make it up to me by doing nice things for me—like you did today— you won't be free. You've done the most wonderful thing in the world for me, but it hasn't made you feel any better, has it?"

"No."

"You don't feel better about it because you haven't *accepted* my forgiveness."

For the first time I dared to look into his face. "I don't understand."

"All you need to do," he explained, "is sincerely

confess your sin and then accept my forgiveness to you. But you've got to reach out and take it before it will be yours. It's the same with God. He offers us the gift of salvation—you know, you've heard me preach—but it does us no good until we accept it."

He turned back to the Joneses' house. "Come on up to my room for tea," he said, and we walked into the house in silence. Slowly, what he was saying to me began to make sense.

After warm, green tea was poured into small, white cups, I told Hudson how sorry I was. And then, like he was saying it all for the first time, Taylor told me that he truly forgave me. As far as he was concerned, what had happened back in the walled city was over, it was dead and buried.

"Thank you," I whispered, tears stinging my eyes, and for the first time since that dreadful night in the strange inland city when I had sold all his possessions, a great weight seemed to roll off my back. It was true! I felt free.

He spent the rest of the evening telling me about all the unsuccessful ways he had tried to meet with Miss Maria Dyer. "But the grim Miss Aldersey was determined to keep us apart. She even made Maria write a letter to me telling me that she never wanted to see me again. That letter broke my heart, but the more I thought about it, the more I couldn't believe it."

"Why not?" I asked.

"I'm not really sure, but the harsh wording in it just didn't seem like the way Maria would say something . . . even if she really didn't want to see me. I went over and over it in my mind, and every time, it sounded more like Miss Aldersey's way of talking. Finally, I got up the courage to secretly send Maria a note asking to speak to her.

"She chose not to meet with me, but one of her friends said that she had *wanted* to but was trying to obey Miss Aldersey. Then the friend said that Maria would meet with me only if God arranged it, and not because of her efforts or mine. I guess that's where you and the waterspout came in," said Taylor. Then he started to laugh, and this time I laughed, too. We laughed until our bellies ached.

❖ ❖ ❖ ❖

Hudson Taylor insisted I stay with him again, this time in the Joneses' house. I continued saving the money I earned from hailing sedan chairs and any other odd job I could get, but the despair of ever saving enough to get home wore me down. The only relief came when I talked to Hudson Taylor about being homesick.

He admitted that he often felt homesick for England, too. That surprised me. I had always thought that because he had chosen to be a missionary and wore Chinese clothes that he wanted to be in China.

"I do want to be in China," he explained. "But that's primarily because God has called me here. That doesn't mean there aren't times when I wish I were back in England. I miss my family deeply."

"But God *hasn't* called me to be here," I pouted, trying to show how my feelings were different and that he couldn't possibly understand how upsetting it was to me to be so far from home.

"Yes," said Taylor. "Well, there are some things we can't understand. But we can pray for a way for you to return."

I knew he was serious the next morning when he insisted that I join him and the Joneses in their prayers, and each person prayed specifically for me.

❖ ❖ ❖ ❖

On March 1, I had been in China exactly one miserable, long year. That day Hudson Taylor burst into the Joneses' kitchen and announced, "Neil! I may have found you a ship home!"

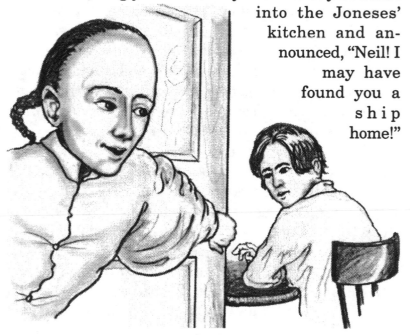

"A ship? How?" I said as I jumped up.

"I met a ship's master, Captain Bowers by name, a fine Christian man. He wants me and another missionary to go south to Swatow, a port city not far from Hong Kong. He says that there is a desperate need for the Gospel there, and he's willing to give us free passage on his ship if we will go."

"But what about me? That's still in China."

"Yes, but it's on the way back to England, and it looks like Captain Bowers might need a cabin boy on the *Geelong*."

The *Geelong* . . . the *Geelong* . . . I knew I had heard that unusual name somewhere before, and then it came to me: The *Geelong* had been one of the first ships to send tea back to England after the prices had gone so high from the war. My heart sank.

"What's the matter?" asked Hudson Taylor. "I thought you would be excited."

"They won't take me," I said. "I almost shipped on the *Geelong* last year, but the agent had heard about me jumping ship from the *Dumfries*, and he was determined to enforce a blackball against me."

"Don't worry," smiled Taylor. "I have already told the captain about the whole thing, and *he's* the one to make the final decision about his crew. You've got a job and a ride home if you want it. We sail before the week's out."

The next two days were filled with excited preparation as I helped Hudson Taylor and his friend gather the supplies they would need for a short-term mission trip to Swatow. I tried to help all I could, especially since Taylor spent every spare minute with Maria—in spite of Miss Aldersey's continued objections.

The evening before our scheduled departure, Miss Dyer was visiting Hudson Taylor at the Joneses' when I happened to walk in on them kissing in the sitting room. Maria jumped back and put her hand to her red face, but Hudson Taylor said, "Excuse us, boy. Now that we are officially engaged, we are sort of making up for lost time, you understand."

That night I hardly slept at all as I reviewed again and again in my mind all the things that had happened to me during the last year and a half. Early in the morning, as a timid grayness crept into the eastern sky, I got out of bed and tiptoed out into the cold March air. For the last time I walked the streets of Shanghai dressed as a Chinese boy.

I was going to tell Namu goodbye. I was going home!

More About Hudson Taylor

J AMES HUDSON TAYLOR was born in 1832 in Barnsley, Yorkshire, England. His strong Christian family was Methodist. In fact, John Wesley was once a guest in his grandparents' home. (See Trailblazer Book, *The Chimney Sweep's Ransom* about John Wesley.)

In his younger years, Hudson was home-schooled and declared an interest in being a missionary to China at the early age of five, but it was not until he was seventeen that he felt he finally understood the Gospel and offered his life to Christ.

Shortly thereafter he went to college to prepare himself as a medical missionary to China. During this time he did his best to begin learning the Mandarin Chinese language.

On September 19, 1853, he set sail for China under the sponsorship of the Chinese Evangelical Society. His trip on the clipper ship *Dumfries* and his first two and a half years in China included all the events related in this book (and more), except that the boy, Neil Thompson, is a fictional character.

In spite of continuing opposition by Miss Aldersey right up to the very day of their wedding, Hudson Taylor and Maria Dyer were happily married on January 20, 1858, . . . with the blessing of Maria's uncle and guardian, Mr. Tarn, of England.

However, it cannot be denied that Hudson Taylor was a very unusual missionary for his day, and that earned him the disapproval of some. Not only did he insist on wearing Chinese clothing (to be better received by the Chinese people), but he believed the Bible taught that we should not get into debt. He was also very impressed by the faith of George Müller (see Trailblazer Book, *The Bandit of Ashley Downs*), the Englishman who, in his lifetime, provided care for ten thousand orphans without asking people for money. Like Müller, Hudson Taylor also believed Christian workers should not ask for money but should rather pray to God about their needs.

As a result of these differences, Hudson Taylor resigned from the Chinese Evangelization Society and continued his mission work on his own. God not only provided all his physical needs, but his ministry among the Chinese people resulted in many converts.

However, in 1860, after exhausting himself as

the director of the London Mission Hospital in Ningpo, China, Taylor became so ill that he and Maria had to return to England. There, he worked on translating the New Testament into the Ningpo Chinese dialect and on recruiting new missionaries for China.

During this time, Taylor's interest in inland China became so strong—spurred on by the memory of his own missionary trips inland—that he founded the China Inland Mission. In 1866, Hudson and Maria and a team of new missionaries sailed back to China to begin new ministries in the interior of the country.

To Taylor's great sorrow, Maria died in 1870 of cholera. This tragedy occurred not long after the Taylors' fifth son, an infant, had died of the same disease. Two years later, Taylor remarried, this time to a Miss Jennie E. Faulding, a leader of the women's ministry in Hangchow.

Under Hudson Taylor's leadership the pioneering of the mission flourished and spread throughout the whole interior of China until, at the time of his retirement in 1901, eight hundred missionaries— nearly half of the evangelical missionaries in China— were with the China Inland Mission. Another notable achievement was that for the first time, these missionaries represented several denominations, all willing to cooperate in the spread of the Gospel.

J. Hudson Taylor died in Changsha in 1905.

For Further Reading

Douglas, J. D., *Who's Who in Christian History* (Wheaton, Ill.: Tyndale House Publishers, Inc., 1962).

Harrison, E. Myers, *Heroes of Faith on Pioneer Trails* (Chicago: Moody Press, 1954).

Pollick, John Charles, *Hudson Taylor and Maria* (New York: McGraw-Hill Book Company, Inc., 1962).

Taylor, J. Hudson, *Hudson Taylor* (an autobiography) (Minneapolis, Minn.: Bethany House Publishers), elsewhere published under the titles, *A Retrospect* (1898) and *To China with Love* (1972).

Thompson, Phyllis, *Hudson Taylor, God's Venturer* (Chicago: Moody Press, 1958).

Tucker, Ruth A., *From Jerusalem to Irian Jaya* (Grand Rapids, Mich.: Zondervan, 1983).